COMING HOME

ANN JOSEPHSON

Zebra Books
Kensington Publishing Corp.
http://www.zebrabooks.com

ZEBRA BOOKS are published by

Kensington Publishing Corp.
850 Third Avenue
New York, NY 10022

Copyright © 2000 by Ann Josephson

All rights reserved. No part of this book may be reproduced in any form or by any means without the prior written consent of the Publisher, excepting brief quotes used in reviews.

If you purchased this book without a cover you should be aware that this book is stolen property. It was reported as "unsold and destroyed" to the Publisher and neither the Author nor the Publisher has received any payment for this "stripped book."

Zebra and the Z logo Reg. U.S. Pat. & TM Off.

First Printing: February, 2000
10 9 8 7 6 5 4 3 2 1

Printed in the United States of America

ONE

Coming home wasn't shaping up to be all Jared Cain had imagined.

Twenty-four years' worth of storms had taken their toll. The cabin where he'd spent the first twelve years of his life was nothing but a pile of rubble, bisected by the rotting skeleton of a tree trunk.

Jared stared at the tree's roots which pointed obscenely toward a brilliant blue sky. He mourned the loss of that black walnut tree. Was the carcass of a tire that rested a few yards away from the ruins the same one his dad had hung from a branch of the tree with a rope?

A touch of color against splintered, graying wood caught his eye. He bent and picked up a filthy square of cloth. A patchwork square. A long-forgotten image of his mother flooded Jared's memory. When they lived here, she'd always had a smile on her face, some piece of needlework in her hands whenever she found a spare minute.

The cabin hadn't been much, but it was the only place Jared associated with home. It was gone now, like Dad, Mom. Everyone except Jared. He'd bought the mountain where he was born and had come here searching.

He looked again at the faded square, noted the precise shapes, the pieces sewn into a pattern of varioussized print rectangles to form the square. His mother had made those tiny stitches, almost invisible and positioned as evenly as if they'd been sewn by machine.

How odd, he reflected, that the only recognizable object that remained from his childhood on Big Bear Mountain should epitomize the precision and control with which he lived his life. Jared started to toss the scrap away, but changed his mind. He tucked it into the pocket of his jeans. His spirits low, he headed back down the mountain.

The summer home he'd had built along the fast-running stream where he used to fish smacked of money, not heart. Its rugged lines and the native stone and cedar blended well with the surroundings. Still, this place was no more home to Jared than the ruins of the old cabin.

He was looking for something. He'd be damned if he knew what it was. Something was missing from his life, something that kept him reaching, seeking some elusive prize that hovered just outside his reach.

He sat on the porch in one of the oak-slat rockers Jim Simmons had just delivered and watched the water rush over jewel-toned rocks in the stream. His dad had believed those stones captured flakes of gold. That he'd find gold nuggets among them.

He laughed. For years he'd tried not to think about that irresponsible, irrepressible man who'd made life seem like a great adventure. His dad had been a dreamer who never believed the gold had played out in these hills of northeast Georgia generations before his time. Jared pictured his dad panning in these streams, certain he'd find the next big strike around the corner.

He'd vowed never to dream, never to leave his family in poverty the way the old man had done when he ran his ancient pickup off an icy mountain road and died. And he hadn't. From the time Jared and his mother moved in with her brother in Atlanta, he'd focused on becoming a success.

He guessed most people would say he'd succeeded, in spite of his broken engagement, his restlessness. Jared cursed his lack of direction, got up, and stood at the porch rail. To keep them still, he stuffed his hands into his pockets.

The seams on that ancient square of cloth abraded his fingertips. Reluctantly, he pulled it out. It was just a scrap. Only a piece of garbage from a past he wouldn't want to revisit even if he could. But he couldn't make himself throw it away. Maybe he'd go see Jim Simmons's sister tomorrow and buy himself a quilt made out of squares like this one.

Darkness came quickly on the mountain. Sighing, Jared sat back down and leaned his head against the cedar wall. He watched the sky turn black but for the brilliant stars and a sliver of a crescent moon. Try as he might, he couldn't banish the sense of emptiness he'd come home to escape.

Althea Simmons hummed a cheerful tune as she quilted around a teddy bear appliqué on the crib quilt she was making for her brother Jim's new baby. As always on weekdays, business was slow.

The little boy they were expecting would round out Jim and Mary's family. He'd certainly make her brother happy.

For a moment Althea stopped stitching. She stared at the rotund teddy bear and mourned for Bill. Mourned that her own dream for home and family had died with him. Ended before it began.

Bill had been gone nearly a year, along with the part of her heart she'd given him back when they were kids. Althea would never again risk loving that much. It had hurt so much to lose the man she'd come to lean on, think of almost as part of herself. Her feelings about Bill's senseless death still hurt too badly for her to think about, much less share, even with her family.

She shook away the pain and regret. She had Jim and his family, friends she'd known all her life, her shop, and the dream she and Bill had shared. The dream she'd vowed not to abandon when she watched the workers lower his coffin into the grave. There was no room in her life for bitterness.

The crunch of tires on gravel drew Althea's gaze to the parking lot. Dark green, low, and sleek, the car was a two-seater, a Mercedes if Althea read the distinctive logo correctly. Unlike most sports cars, it had a substantial look about it. Still, the car seemed insignificant when compared with the man who emerged from it.

Long, lean, as graceful as a mountain cat, he sauntered toward her door. Althea's heart beat faster. When he stepped across the threshold and met her gaze, her cheeks grew warm.

Every cell in her body prickled with awareness. Althea told herself her reaction was to the look of loneliness in his eyes. As expressive as their color was ambiguous, they were brown or forest green, depending upon the angle from which she viewed them. They bespoke emptiness, an emotion all too familiar to her.

Dark hair that could use a trim rippled slightly in the breeze and drew her attention to a face that was all masculine angles, from strong jaw line to a classic Roman nose that looked as if it might have been broken a time or two. A face she might have seen on an ad for camping gear or formal wear.

"Ms. Simmons?"

How did this man know her name? "Yes?"

"I'm Jared Cain. Your brother Jim has been making some chairs for me. When I mentioned yesterday that I'd like a quilt, he said to come see you."

If Althea hadn't known better, she would have sworn the man who had recently bought Big Bear Mountain was suffering. But Jared Cain had no reason to be sad, if the local realtor could be believed. According to her, this man had everything anyone could possibly want.

Except, apparently, a quilt. "I'll be glad to show you what I have," she said, forcing herself to focus on business. "Come in."

"Jim told me you make the finest quilts in these hills." Jared ran his fingers across a point of the Lone Star quilt on the rack next to the door. "Do you have one like this?"

He reached into his pocket and brought out a quilt block time and the elements had all but destroyed. He passed it to Althea.

"Not exactly." She couldn't immediately identify the pattern. It looked similar to a Log Cabin, and she thought at first it might be a variation on that familiar design. When she turned the block over, though, she noticed that its construction differed from the classic Log Cabin's.

"It's similar to that one," she said, pointing out the Log Cabin quilt draped over a miniature bed on the other side of the room.

He walked over and looked at the quilt, then turned back to Althea. "I found that square in the ruins of the cabin where I was born. This quilt is nice, but I want one made out of squares like the one in your hand."

His crooked smile warmed her, gave her a tingly feeling. "Why?" she asked.

"Because my mother started making one like that years ago, before we moved to Atlanta. She never got the chance to finish it."

Althea saw the faraway look in his eyes. Silently she encouraged him to go on.

"She said the geese would fly away from the mountains, the way we were going to do, but that someday they'd come back. Appropriate, don't you think, for a wanderer who has finally come home?" His tone was casual—too casual, Althea thought when she met his hooded gaze.

Suddenly she remembered the pattern, an unusual one she'd once seen at a mountain craft exhibition in Dahlonega. "Flying Geese in the Cabin," she said.

"Excuse me?"

"That's the name of this pattern."

Jared looked at the square she'd set on a table, then at Althea. His expression was solemn, intense. "Can you make me a quilt like this one?"

How could she refuse when he made her believe this quilt would mean much more to him than an accessory to decorate his bedroom or a cover to keep him warm?

"Yes." If she couldn't find a pattern for Flying Geese, she could make one from the block he'd found.

"How soon?"

How like a man! "Depends."

"On what?"

"Lots of things. How many other jobs I have to finish before I can start your quilt. Who I can find to help me with the piecing." Althea motioned for Jared to come closer to the quilting frame. When he complied, she showed him the tiny hand stitches that went into quilting each section of the crib quilt. "It takes about two hundred hours to make a full size quilt, after the top is finished."

He shrugged. "My bed's king-size." His tone was deep, his drawl muted.

Althea hoped her cheeks didn't look as hot as they felt. What was it about this man that made her envision him stretched out naked across a massive bed, his lean, fit body framed with the vibrant patchwork of a handmade quilt?

"Ms. Simmons?"

He must think she was a complete ninny. "I'm sorry. Do you want to use your quilt as a bedspread or a coverlet?"

He looked confused. "What's the difference?"

"A bedspread goes all the way to the floor. A coverlet stops where the dust ruffle begins." He still had a perplexed look, so she showed him some photos. "Do you want the quilt to cover to the floor or do you want to have a dust ruffle?"

"No ruffles."

She should have known without asking. Jared Cain didn't appear to be the ruffle type. Silently she calculated the time it would take her to make such a large quilt. "I should be able to finish it for you by September."

"That's three months from now." He sounded surprised.

Apparently the man thought she had nothing to do but labor over his quilt. "Summer is my busiest time in the shop, Mr. Cain."

"Jared."

A sexy name. A sexy man. Just the sound of his voice implied intimacy. "Would you like to pick the materials out today?"

He glanced around the room. When his gaze settled on the two walls that were lined with bolts of fabric, he shook his head. "That could take some thinking," he told her, as if overwhelmed by the variety of colors and prints.

"After you pick the colors you like, the choices will be narrowed down quite a bit." Althea couldn't help smiling at the relieved look on Jared's arresting face.

"Dark green," he said without hesitation.

She should have guessed. His car was that deep, almost black shade of green. His polo shirt sported a wide band of forest green, with narrower stripes of navy blue and gray against a white background.

Before she realized how much time had passed, they had spent nearly two hours selecting the solid forest green background color and a dozen or so mostly geometric prints in coordinating colors. She was ready to make a pattern from the block Jared's mother had cut and pieced more than twenty years ago.

She explained how she'd make the first block and show it to him for his approval. Afterward, she'd hire one or two mountain women to do the cutting and piecing of the forty-eight twelve-inch blocks that would make the center of the quilt. When the piecing was done, she'd begin the hand-quilting process.

She'd work as quickly as possible. As unlikely as it seemed, Althea had a feeling this quilt might give Jared Cain a little of the feeling of home she sensed he was missing. She hoped so. She wanted to chase away the sadness in his eyes.

"Thanks," Jared said a few minutes later as he paused in the doorway of Althea's shop. "Could I interest you in showing me around these mountains? It's been years since I was here."

"If I'm going to get your quilt finished when I said I would, I'm not going to have much time to play tour guide."

He didn't know why, but this quiet woman made him feel comfortable. Sensually aware, too, the way no woman had affected him for a long time. At home. He hadn't felt that way anywhere lately—not at work, and not at his Atlanta condo. Not even on Big Bear Mountain, which he'd bought for the singular purpose of coming home.

Althea wasn't a beauty like Marcie. Hell, she wasn't even particularly pretty, compared with some of the women he saw every day in Atlanta. She was—well, average. Average height and weight, light brown hair. Nice body, nice face. Nothing spectacular or even out of the ordinary.

Jared wasn't certain what it was that drew him to

her, only that he was drawn—more than he'd been toward a woman for years.

He met her gaze, liked the twinkle he detected in pale blue eyes that reminded him of a clear morning sky. "I could wait a couple of extra weeks for my quilt."

"You sounded awfully anxious to have it quickly, a few minutes ago."

"Maybe I've changed my mind."

"We'll see."

Jared wasn't used to being put off. He didn't much like the feeling it left in him. "When will I see you again?"

"Sometime in the next few days. I'll need to come up to your place, see the spot where you're going to put your quilt so I can decide what sort of border will work best."

Jared liked the idea of having Althea in his cabin. There was something wholesome—almost innocent—about her. A quality he couldn't deny, although he'd have been hard-pressed to define it. He also liked the way her very ordinary features combined to form a pleasant, interesting composite.

"You're welcome anytime."

"I should probably come soon, before I get too far along with the cutting and piecing. How about next Monday?"

"Sure. Why don't you wait until after you close the shop, so you can stay awhile? I'll fix us a bite to eat."

When she smiled, her whole face lit up. "Would around six o'clock be all right?"

"Fine. Do you know how to get there?"

"Sure. Don't you know you've been the major source

of gossip for the last six months, since you went and bought yourself that entire mountain?" When she teased him, her face lit up, made her look sexy. Almost beautiful. "Hey, thanks for the business."

That, Jared realized, was his cue to leave. "Anytime. See you Monday," he replied. Then he turned, headed for his car.

For the first time since he'd walked out of his Atlanta office a week ago, Jared felt a sense of purpose. As precisely as he'd ever designed a game move or plotted the marketing strategy for a new Cain Software game or utility, he planned the simple kind of meal he felt certain he could cook.

In Blairsville, he bought a set of matching dishes, then shopped for groceries. When he got home, he set himself to cleaning his elaborate mountain hideaway. Monday would come sooner if he kept himself occupied with something other than taking care of business.

The hum of the vacuum cleaner as it sucked dust from the huge braided rugs on the floors of highly polished hardwood planks, the swishing noise from the dishwasher, and the drone of the gas generator outside mingled in a cacophony that reminded Jared of the city he'd left behind.

One by one, the sounds of civilization dropped away, except for the quiet hum of the generator. Jared had put it in so he'd never be without electricity, but this was the first time he'd noticed its intrusive sound. Its humming rang in his ears, then faded when he stepped onto the porch.

The generator's hum blended into the sound of water rushing along the stream bed, tumbling down the mountain toward the river. An occasional bird squawked from high in the fragrant cedar trees outside.

Memories of Althea's soft voice washed over Jared. Those memories fed a sensual image of lovers tangled in soft cotton sheets, beneath a quilt made by her soft, talented hands. Monday was going to be a long time coming.

TWO

"This place. It's—magnificent. Jim told me, but he doesn't have the same way with words that he has with his wood." Althea looked first at the cabin, then settled her gaze on the stream that passed under the porch, beneath her feet.

"Different, isn't it?"

"I love everything about this place. The setting. The stream outside your door. The house itself. Everything fits, as if this house were meant to be right here."

For the first time since he'd seen the finished product, Jared didn't regret having left the design of the place to the Atlanta architect whose vision of a simple mountain hideaway hadn't exactly meshed with his own. "Glad you like it," he said. "Come on inside."

He stepped back to let Althea go first. She set her big quilted tote bag on one of the sofas, then glanced at the blank walls and the empty mantel over the massive stone fireplace. "When did you move in?" she asked.

"Last week. It's still pretty bare." No barer than the Atlanta condo where he'd been living for the past ten years, he reminded himself. "Guess I'm not much for collecting things. Come on back. We're going to eat in the kitchen."

He'd warmed ham and green beans, made scalloped potatoes from a boxed mix. Better unimaginative, he'd told himself when he planned the menu, than disastrous. "Have a seat," he said, as he held a chair for her. "I'll put the food on the table."

She ate some of everything, and the food tasted fine to him, so Jared figured he'd chosen well. As dinner partners went, Althea was on the quiet end of the spectrum, which he didn't mind. It left him free to enjoy the faint, sweet smell of her cologne and observe the way she held her fork. Her tongue darted out the corner of her mouth every now and then to capture an errant crumb.

"Coffee?" he asked, the pot poised over a big ironstone mug.

She shook her head. "I'd never get to sleep."

"Tea? A soft drink?"

"I'm fine. Shouldn't we take a look at—"

"My bedroom? Come on upstairs. I'll show you." He set down the coffeepot, strode through the living room to the circular wrought-iron staircase in the entryway.

She paused in the doorway to the master suite, then took a step inside. "Oh, my. Jim made that bed frame, didn't he?"

"Yes. I wanted that bed the minute I saw it." The rugged-looking oak boards that held the king-size mattress and box springs . . . the heavy carved oak headboard . . . and soaring posters that lent strength and balance to the piece. It had caught his eye and drawn him into her brother's woodworking shop outside Dahlonega last summer, soon after he'd bought Big Bear Mountain from a developer gone bust.

"It's perfect. When he made this bed, I never thought that it would actually fit in somebody's bedroom."

"This room would hold a couple of them." Jared didn't know whether he should feel complimented or embarrassed, but he leaned toward the embarrassed side. Mountain folk didn't usually have the kind of money it took to build a place like his, and the few who did didn't generally flaunt it. "I never realized until this place was halfway finished that it was going to be so big. Guess I should have paid more attention to my architect, kept him from going berserk."

"Oh, no. I've never seen a place so—so at one with its surroundings. Jared, your quilt is going to look lovely in here." She stepped over to the bed and smoothed the dark green blanket, then propped his pillow against the headboard before moving toward the huge plate-glass window that overlooked the porch.

When she looked out at the breathtaking mountain vista, she sighed. "I could get used to seeing this every morning when I wake up."

Jared could get used to seeing her first thing in the morning, all sleepy-eyed and warm in his arms. No. He squashed that picture. He didn't think that way. Never had. He'd never thought of himself as particularly sensual, never been one to chase skirts. Marcie had called him a boring lover, and he guessed he might have been, at least with her.

He had to get out of here. Had to quit thinking with parts of his anatomy that had never before been so unruly. "Do you need to measure, or anything?" he asked.

Her smile when she turned and met his gaze sent blood slamming south. "No. The bed's standard king-size, standard height. I made the quilt Jim displayed on it at the shop."

"It had flowers." Big red poppies and green leaves, he recalled, on a white background. It had reminded him of Christmas, not his favorite holiday.

"I know. After Jim brought the quilt back to my shop, I sold it to a lady from Nashville."

She didn't sound upset that he hadn't bought the quilt along with the bed. "Shall we go downstairs? I could build a fire." He wanted to keep her here longer—as long as he could.

She moved toward the door instead of the living room, paused. "I really have to be going."

"Humor me. You still haven't told me what's going on around here—what someone who's been away for over twenty years might like to see."

Hand on the doorknob, she smiled. "There are all sorts of events we locals put on to part you city slickers from your cash. Everything from helicopter rides to tubing down the rivers. Speaking of tubing, there's the Fourth of July Festival in Helen next week. It's on the Chattahoochee River. Tubing's great there. They do German and Bavarian foods and have a big craft show. I never miss it if I can help it."

"Sounds like fun. Can I tag along?"

For a minute he thought she might say no. Then she nodded. "I'd like that. Jared, I do have to go now."

He watched the lights of her Pathfinder until they disappeared around the first curve in the mountain road. When he went inside, he felt Althea's presence as if she were still there.

* * *

It was almost as if Jared were there, Althea thought the next morning at her shop as she laid out stacks of the triangles and rectangles she'd just cut for his quilt. Looking at a subdued print of blueberries and their leaves against a cream background, she recalled how she'd had to coax him to pick these lighter prints that would make up half of each of the Flying Geese blocks.

Jared was darkness, not light. The forest green solid fabrics and the navy and dark green geometric designs had been easy for him to choose from the dozens of fabric bolts she'd shown him after he selected the basic colors. Althea stacked dark pieces next to the lights, sketched the combinations to be pieced, and noted how many blocks there should be of each variation.

She sighed. Flying Geese wasn't a particularly complex pattern, but it had to be pieced just right. Good thing Trina Wells had time on her hands now, before the blackberries started to get ripe.

There Trina was, outside. The distinctive wheeze of her old pickup truck was as good as an announcement. "Hey, Trina," Althea called out when she heard the door open.

"Morning. Is that coffee I smell?"

Althea motioned toward the pot on a little table in the corner. "Have some. I made it fresh, just for you."

"Thanks. A good thing it was, you called me now. In a couple more weeks, I'll be up to my elbows in blackberry jelly." Trina filled a mug with coffee, then dumped in a generous helping of sugar. "So, this is going to be the king-size bedspread?" she asked when she joined Althea at the counter.

"Uh-huh."

"The woman must have more money than sense."

"It's for a man. Jared Cain. Did you know him when he lived here before?"

Trina raised herself up to her full height, which Althea figured must be close to six feet. All angles and jutting bones, her body seemed at odds with her round face, bright blue eyes, and full lips that curved upward in a cherubic smile.

"My ma recalls his folks. Said his pa was a good-looking devil, good for nothing like so many men that's easy on the eyes. Jared's a lot younger than me, older than my kids. I guess he must've been starting school about the time I was quitting. What's he like?"

"He's a good-looking devil, same as your ma described his pa. Dark-haired, tall. Lean. You wouldn't forget him if the two of you ever met. Come on, this quilt of his isn't likely to piece itself."

Trina sat in front of an old-fashioned sewing machine and adjusted her chair. After draining her mug, she set it aside and studied the sample block Althea had made. "Looks like a Log Cabin, but it ain't."

"No. It's called Flying Geese in the Cabin. While you piece, I'm going to finish this." Althea sat in front of the quilting frame and picked up a threaded needle. "If I don't get busy, Jim and Mary's baby will be here before his quilt's finished."

The low whir of the sewing machine penetrated the silence, filled Althea's mind as she made the tiny stitches around the last of the teddy bear appliqués.

"Time for a break?" she asked after they'd worked for several hours, knowing that if she didn't say something, Trina would sit at that machine until she dropped.

"Can't say I'd mind another cup of coffee." The older woman stood. She shook herself, as if the motion would get the kinks out of all those bones and joints. "You want some of my jelly to sell in here this year?"

"Absolutely."

Trina and her husband Joe lived on the side of a mountain not far from Lake Winfield Scott, where blackberry thickets abounded. She'd been braving the brambles, picking those berries and making jelly, every summer for as long as Althea could remember. How much money had she made? Althea had no idea, but she'd heard that Trina fiercely guarded the profits she kept in her kitchen in a big ironstone butter churn.

Althea had no doubt Trina's profits had been depleted from time to time over the years when Joe got laid off at the mine or that most of the money she'd make for piecing Jared's quilt would go toward keeping Little Joe, her youngest, in the divinity college in Chattanooga. Like most of the women around here, Trina worked hard, yet got little personal gain from her labor. Unlike some, Trina seemed happy with her lot.

"How's the plan coming for your co-op?" Trina asked when she'd refilled her mug and settled back in the chair in front of the sewing machine.

Althea shrugged. "Slowly. The idea kind of lost momentum, when Bill died. He'd been pushing for help from local businessmen to buy land and build or fix up a place for us to start out. Bankers don't seem anxious to listen, now that it's me doing the asking."

"Bill was a real good boy. Shame it was he had to die, especially for nothing more important than to arrest the likes of Buck Dillard and his kin for making a fresh batch of white lightning."

A little over a year had passed since she'd held Bill's hand at the hospital while he lost his fight to live. Althea still hurt when she thought of him and the plans they'd made. The dreams that went up in smoke the day the sheriff sent Bill and two other deputies to help the federal treasury men close down a still on Dillard Creek.

Althea felt a tear work its way down her cheek. Angrily, she brushed it away. She was alive. Bill wouldn't want her burying herself with him. He'd been one of the good ones, the ones doomed to die too young.

The sound of Trina's voice permeated Althea's thoughts. "What?"

"You gotta get on with living, girl. Find yourself a new man. Kick up your heels. Lordy, you're still a young thing, too young to dry up and blow away with grieving."

Althea smiled. Trina meant well. "I'm not drying up and blowing away. I've got the shop, and my teaching job. And I'm not about to give up on the co-op. It's just going to take me longer to get the backing, without Bill."

"None of those things are going to keep you warm on a winter night."

Althea's gaze settled on the growing stack of quilt blocks. Jared. The way he'd turned her warm and liquid with nothing more than a heated look, Althea had no doubt he'd become a furnace if they were ever alone together in a bed, winter or summer. There was something about him . . .

"You know I'm right. If you don't quit grieving, find yourself a new man, you'll dry up and blow away. Ain't right, a nice woman like you goin' through life all alone."

"Jared's taking me to the festival in Helen." The words came out before Althea could bite them back.

"You're sweet on him, aren't you, girl?"

"Excuse me?"

"Jared Cain. The poor boy turned rich city slicker. The one who bought Big Bear Mountain. Built himself a fancy place. Ordered up this here quilt from you. You look at the blocks I just sewed up as if they were the man himself, stripped naked and served up on a platter like a Christmas turkey."

"I don't—"

Trina laughed. "You do. You may not realize it, but you've got the look. The look a woman gets when she wants a man."

"Trina, I hardly know Jared."

"Don't take a whole lot of knowing, just wanting. I remember me, first time I laid eyes on Joe. Knew I wanted him right then and there. Of course, I held onto myself till I could drag him in front of the preacher. Might never have trapped him, otherwise." Trina laughed, drained her mug. "You sure do make good coffee."

"Thanks. But I am not lusting after Jared Cain. I'm making him a quilt. That's all."

But Althea wondered if that were true. After all, she'd gone to his place, and she'd agreed to let him join her for the Fourth of July celebration in Helen. He certainly did make her want things she hadn't thought about since Bill died.

"If you say so." Trina turned back to the sewing machine, picked up another tiny triangle.

Later, after Trina had gone, Althea sat in the shop long after she should have closed up and gone home.

Thoughts tumbled through her mind—of the boy she'd loved since seventh grade . . . and the man who had captured her fantasies when he walked in and asked her to make him a quilt.

THREE

Jared remembered being by himself in the mountains years ago, but not feeling isolated—totally alone, the way he felt tonight. A gentle creak of new oak wood punctuated each backward motion of his rocker against the porch floorboards.

Stars twinkled. How many millions of them were up there, he wouldn't venture a guess. Their numbers humbled him, made him realize what a tiny part he played in the world as a whole.

A night bird chirped from down the road. The cheery sound made Jared smile. He sipped his beer as he pictured Althea in her shop, in his bedroom, and in her beat-up Pathfinder last night, as she got ready to trek down Big Bear Mountain to the cabin she called home.

He was insane. This wasn't his world now. Althea Simmons wasn't the kind of woman who attracted him, the kind he lusted after. Hell, he didn't lust after any woman. He hadn't for longer than he could recall.

Why was it that he was thinking about a woman too young and too country, too ordinary to interest him—when he had hardly been able to dredge up the interest to make love with Marcie the last six months they were together?

Jared sighed. He should have been inside, checking out a new game one of his programmers was certain would be the next Pac-Man. He needed to evaluate it and two other programs his assistant had E-mailed for his approval.

Unfortunately, all he seemed to be able to concentrate on was Althea Simmons. Her sweet face. Her soft drawl. Her full breasts where he'd like to lay his head. Her talented hands, hands he imagined caressing him instead of the soft materials they'd selected to make his quilt.

He got up, moved to the edge of the porch, and stared into the pervasive darkness. Rushing water in the stream, punctuated by night creatures' calls, broke the silence but didn't ease the need he felt for human company. For a woman he'd just met. A woman who was totally wrong for him. Althea.

Marcie had been right. Beautiful, bright, and as ambitious for Cain Software's success as he'd been. So, why hadn't they married? Why weren't they together now, running his company and raising a family? Jared turned away from the night and went inside.

He sat down at the computer and loaded the new game his assistant was so hot about. As he played, he tried to sort out his feelings.

He couldn't blame Marcie for dumping him. Five years was a long time for her to have spent engaged to a man who couldn't say "I love you." At the end, they'd even lost the friendship on which they'd based their long relationship. When that was gone, there had been nothing left.

When she broke their engagement five months ago, Marcie had also resigned as marketing director for his company. Jared's biggest regret was that he was having the devil's own time replacing her at the office. He was fairly certain that didn't speak well for him as a human being.

What would Marcie have thought of this new game? Jared played it again. He could practically hear her wax poetic about the prospects of launching an ad campaign featuring the game's flamboyant pirate hero, Captain Morgan.

Scratch that name. He made a mental note to have his assistant tell the programmer to rename his swashbuckler. No need to risk a lawsuit from the manufacturer of the rum of the same name. Marcie would have caught that potential problem first time through.

He shut off the computer and stretched out across his bed. When he imagined a woman lying there with him, it was Althea who came to mind.

On the morning of the Fourth of July, Althea put on red shorts over her bathing suit, then slipped on a white sleeveless shirt and tied its tails at her waist. It had been so long since she'd had occasion to dress for a day outdoors, she'd had to dig deep in her closet to find the right clothes.

Since last year's festival had been held just a few days after Bill's funeral, she hadn't gone. She picked up a photo from her dresser and stared at it. It was hard, but she tried to remember how Bill had smiled. She'd loved him so much. He'd been alive and vital one minute, then dead the next.

She set the photo down. Regret wouldn't go away, but she pushed it to the back of her mind.

The last thing Bill would have wanted was for her to wither up and die even though her heart still beat. He'd have wanted her to find someone new and be happy. She couldn't, though. Couldn't risk falling in love, hurting again the way she had since he'd been gone.

She'd have fun today. She'd enjoy the festival with Jared Cain, ride in his fancy car and let the wind blow her hair. If he asked, she'd kiss him. Maybe she'd do even more. After all, she didn't want to fall in love. Who could be a safer lover than a stranger, too rich and citified to want more than a summer fling with a country girl like her?

Althea heard the low purr of an engine, glanced out her bedroom window. Her pulse raced at the sight of Jared. When she opened the front door and met his gaze, she couldn't help but notice how different he looked today, as if he'd shrugged off whatever cares had weighted him down last week.

"Are you ready?" he asked.

Althea picked up the canvas tote bag she'd packed with suntan lotion, a towel, and a change of clothes. "Ready as I'll ever be." She followed Jared outside, locked the door behind her.

She was no Cinderella, and Jared's sleek convertible was no pumpkin-turned-coach. With the wind whipping her hair and the Mercedes sports coupe's powerful engine roaring in her ears, though, Althea thought she might pass for a fairy-tale princess. Jared drove fast but skillfully around hairpin curves on the narrow state highway that led to Helen and the festival.

They parked in one of the lots near the river, then strolled aimlessly among the throng of tourists. Jared acted like a kid, sampling goodies from every vendor they passed.

His good humor rubbed off on Althea. She was happy today—happy to be with him and happier to feel alive. Part of a good-natured crowd, they wandered along Union Street, sipping peach cider and munching boiled peanuts.

"Look over there." Jared gestured toward the middle of the river, toward laughing tourists in fat tire tubes bouncing over the rapids. She followed his gaze across the river, where more people were flocking to rent rafts and inner tubes.

Althea stretched her legs to match Jared's longer stride and breathed in the cool, fresh mountain air. "Looks as if they're having fun," she said. She knew she was enjoying herself.

Following the bend in the river, they peered in windows of shops that offered crafts, antiques, and collectibles. "Want to go take a closer look?" Jared asked when Althea paused to look at an antique quilt in the window of one of the stores.

"That's all right. The pattern's one I know." She smiled when she looked up to meet his gaze.

"Okay." He looked across the winding road toward the fast-moving Chattahoochee River. "Want to go tubing?"

"I wondered if you'd ever ask." Suddenly she wanted to be alone with him, away from the crowd. What better way than to float with him down the river? The chilly water might cool the heat in his glittering green-gold gaze. With luck, it would squelch the fire that threatened to erupt in her.

She pictured them caught up in a strong current, careening down the river toward a distant pickup point. Out of control. No more so, though, than the way Jared was making her feel.

He took her hand and headed toward a tube vendor who seemed a little less harried than the rest. After Jared picked tubes for them, and an extra one to hold the six-pack of soft drinks he'd bought, he lashed all three tubes together.

Althea was glad. She hadn't relished taking a solitary trip, where she might end up a long way away from Jared, caught up in rapids that could get a little intimidating.

He stripped off his shoes, shirt, and jeans, revealing a surprisingly muscular chest dappled with soft, dark hair that arrowed past his navel to disappear into snug-fitting navy swim trunks. Althea squelched a sigh. He was gorgeous all over.

"Want to take off some clothes?" he asked, apparently unaware she couldn't take her eyes off him.

Automatically, her hands went to her midriff. Her gaze still fixed on his broad shoulders, she untied her shirt. When she'd taken it off and stepped out of her shorts, she pried off her tennis shoes one at the time, then stuffed her clothes into her tote bag. Her cheeks grew warm when she realized he was staring at her, too.

He took her carryall, then stuffed it and his own gym bag into a rusty locker. "Ready?"

"I'm ready." Althea plunged into the shallow river, not waiting for Jared to launch the tubes. "Ouch," she cried at the first contact of the icy water with her shivering legs.

"Ouch, yourself. It'll warm up." Laughing, Jared

pushed the tubes into the water and settled Althea into her side. He took his place inside the biggest of the tubes. "Ready?"

"Yes."

He pushed them off the bank into deeper water. They kicked until they reached midstream, where a gentle current took over. It drew them along the river at an easy pace.

He reached over their extra tube and took her hand. Despite the ice-cold water, his palm and fingers felt warm, and much harder than she'd expected. He must have personally split those logs she'd seen on the woodpile at his place on Big Bear Mountain.

Althea wanted to prolong the contact, so she made no move to withdraw her hand. "What do you remember about living on the mountain when you were a boy?" she asked.

"My mom's smile."

He paused, then painted a picture Althea had seen too often, of a family barely scraping by, poor on everything but love. A family that had been decimated when fate took its breadwinner out of the picture. A mother not able to cope on her own, forced to seek out her kin to care for her and Jared after his father died.

They talked as they floated down the river. "Why did you come back, Jared?"

He closed his eyes, then opened them and met her gaze. He smiled, then shrugged. "Damned if I know. We were dirt poor. Wouldn't have been a whole lot better off if Dad had lived, I don't guess. He lived chasing a rainbow—always looking for a big gold strike on that pathetic little piece of Big Bear Mountain he called his own. Wouldn't listen when folks reminded him no one had found more than a gram or so of gold dust around there in more than fifty years."

Althea smiled. "You were happy on the mountain, weren't you?"

"I guess I was. I had an old tire swing, and plenty of room to explore. Mom was content, keeping up that ramshackle cabin and catering to Dad. I guess I came back here looking for . . ." His voice trailed off, as if he were caught up in thought. "Hey, enough about me. Tell me how you happened to open a quilt shop right down the road from Big Bear Mountain."

Should she tell Jared about Bill? About the plans they'd made? Althea hesitated. It still hurt to think of him, but she'd promised herself she would enjoy living the way she knew Bill would have wanted.

"I was born and raised in the cabin behind the shop. My father preached at the little church up the road. Never thought much about leaving."

She paused, pulled her hand back. For a moment she stared at the water ahead, watched the froth that formed as it tumbled over big boulders in the riverbed.

"Everything I wanted was here. My family, friends. The boy I'd loved since seventh grade. We'd been engaged since my junior year in college."

"Past tense?"

"He got killed last year." The boulders lurked in front of them. She had to paddle hard or she'd have scraped herself on their jagged edges.

Jared grabbed a floating limb and used it to push them farther away from the boulders. "I'm sorry," he said, his tone conveying deeper emotion than his words.

Suddenly she wanted to tell Jared the dreams she'd shared with Bill, dreams she'd vowed to keep alive. She looked at Jared, then let him take her hand again. The water was calm now, deep and crystal clear. Here, with no one except the two of them around, other than the trout and whatever animals might be hiding along the riverbank, she felt at peace.

She talked about Bill, about how all he'd wanted to do was help the people he loved. Tears spilled down her cheeks, put a salt taste into her mouth when she told Jared about the plans they'd made for a good life together and the dream they'd shared, to help mountain women achieve financial independence with the crafts they'd been doing all their lives.

Jared reached out to her. With the pad of his thumb, he brushed a tear from her cheek. He didn't seem to mind sharing her pain. "What happened to him?" he asked.

"Bill was a deputy sheriff. He and two other deputies went with some treasury agents to break up a moonshine operation on Dillard Creek, northeast of Dahlonega. Buck Dillard shot him dead—wounded a treasury agent and one of the other deputies."

Jared's compelling eyes registered shock. He started to speak, then apparently changed his mind.

"You've obviously been away from here a long time," she said. "Like poverty and gold fever, moonshine has always been around in these mountains. Probably always will be."

"My dad used to bring a jug home every now and then. God, violence is everywhere." Jared sounded disillusioned, as if he'd expected to find safe haven where none existed.

" 'Fraid so. Anyhow, now Bill is dead, and I'm still

here, trying to carry on the way he'd have wanted me to."

"How old are you, Althea?"

"Twenty-seven. Why?"

Jared shook his head. "I've got nine years on you, honey. You're too young to have experienced so much pain. Come on, smile for me. I promise I won't make you cry again today." Shaking his head, he reached into the sling inside the middle tube and grabbed two sodas. "Here, drink this."

She sipped her drink. Jared was the only constant in a scene that changed slowly, then faster as they came to spots in the river where the current ran strong. Bright green leaves on overhanging branches. Blankets of wildflowers in shades of lavender and gold along the banks, and boulders tossed along the shore by storm-fed waters some time in the distant past.

A panorama of nature, and a man. Suddenly Althea wanted this man to teach her all the mysteries she and Bill had saved for the wedding night fate had denied them. The thought shamed her, but it wouldn't go away, no matter how hard she tried to squelch it.

The wind blew through the trees, made Althea shiver as Jared helped her onto the bank at the pickup point. His smile was contagious, his presence warming. By the time they finished a ride on a rickety truck back to the tube vendor where they'd begun their trip, Althea felt good again.

They stopped on Main Street at the WurstHaus for a spicy bratwurst sandwich. Lively accordion music and strong imported beer combined to raise Althea's spirits. When they left to go back to Jared's car, she laughed with him at the antics of a little boy chasing a colorful butterfly along the riverbank.

On the way home, Althea explained how she and Bill had hoped the craft co-op they wanted to build could give mountain homemakers the chance to earn a living from skills they'd had since childhood. Not wanting to spoil the carefree mood, she didn't tell him how the project's support from the business community seemed to have died with Bill. Still, Jared's enthusiastic response to the co-op idea encouraged her, and his suggestions about financing and management made her feel she might find an ally in him.

The co-op had been Bill's dream as much as hers. As she felt the wind in her hair, Jared's body radiating warmth within the confines of his sports car, Althea couldn't help feeling a twinge of guilt. But she couldn't help feeling more alive than she had since Bill died.

Twilight had fallen by the time Jared stopped in front of Althea's cabin. The setting sun cast an eerie glow across his handsome face and lent him an air of mystery. A sense of danger.

She looked into eyes that had looked green-gold, now appeared dark brown, glittered with shards of gold. The current she'd felt the first time she saw him grew stronger. Her body began to tingle. Although his lips curved in a smile, there was an intensity in his gaze that fascinated her. Sent a momentary chill of fear down her spine.

With one hand he cupped her chin, while he drew her so close, she could feel his heart beat through the layers of their clothes. She smelled the coffee he'd drunk after the dinner they'd shared at a country restaurant near Raven Creek Falls.

How would the sandpapery shadow of dark beard on his cheeks feel against the sensitive skin of her neck? She didn't have long to wonder, because he dipped his head and captured her lips. His kiss was so soft and so gentle, it might have been a prayer—or a promise.

FOUR

Promise. He'd never felt this way before, as if his very existence depended on getting as close to a woman as a man could get, drinking of the heady mix of passion and innocence he tasted on her lips.

With Althea he could fly. On a visceral level, he knew this woman, wanted her, sought her special elixir to make himself whole. Jared deepened the kiss, drew her tighter into his embrace, tangled his hand in the soft silk of her hair.

With his tongue, he tried to coax her to let him in. Her lips yielded, softened beneath his. With small hands she caressed his chest, made him want more. Then she trembled.

He must be moving too fast, scaring her. With regret, he broke the kiss, held her at arm's length.

When she looked up at him, he noticed the deep flush on her cheeks. Her breathing was ragged when she tried to speak. "I . . ." The words apparently wouldn't come.

"Enjoyed it?" Jared reined in his body's unruly reaction.

"Yes. Why'd you stop?"

"Because you trembled."

She stepped back, then ran her fingers through her hair. "I should be mortified. I hardly know you."

"I feel as though we've known each other forever." And he did. He couldn't put it in words, but he'd sensed it from the first, a connection with Althea that had nothing to do with how long or how deeply they'd been acquainted.

With one hand she reached out and stroked his cheek. "Still—"

"You feel it, too." He caught her hand, then brushed it across his lips.

"Yes. I feel it."

The way she worried her lower lip between her teeth, she could have been a child. No child had ever made Jared ache like this, though. "When can I see you again?" he asked, his body trembling with desire.

"Call me." Her voice was husky.

He met her gaze. Her eyes were bright, full of promise. "All right. Dream happy dreams," he said. He wanted to kiss her again, but feared that if he did, he wouldn't be able to let her go. Softly, he tucked a wayward strand of hair behind her ear. Then he stepped back and let her go inside.

After she closed the door, he strode to his car. Damn! He'd never wanted a woman so much.

What was it about Althea? She was no seductress, yet she'd seduced him. Beneath her aura of innocence, Jared glimpsed the promise of a sensual woman—a woman he wanted to discover. A woman he sensed could fill the empty spaces in his dreams.

* * *

She felt empty. Not since the day of Bill's funeral had Althea felt so alone. She lay in bed and ached. She shouldn't have let Jared put her off. If she hadn't hesitated, she could have been in his arms now. She could have been living the joys she'd glimpsed but never fully experienced with Bill.

Sitting up, she turned on a lamp on the table by the bed. Bill's solemn face stared at her from its oak frame. Althea pulled the other pillow over, arranged it against the headboard, and leaned back. For the first time in months, she let bittersweet memories have full rein.

Why had Bill insisted that they wait? Why had he denied them both the pleasure of consummating their love? Althea had no doubt he'd wanted her. She recalled nights when she'd felt him get hard inside his clothes. He'd touched her breasts, and made her want much more.

Fire came to her cheeks when she remembered how she'd begged him to ease the throbbing ache he'd caused deep in her belly. Suddenly she was furious. Bill had been a fool, holding out for a wedding night that would never be. Now she'd never know if making love with him would have fulfilled the sensual promise of his touch.

She set the photo down. When she recalled Bill saying the wait would make their wedding night sweeter, she laughed out loud. He'd been so wrong when he'd said God would reward them for waiting until they said their vows. Many times in the last year, Althea had wanted to scream, to rail at God for taking Bill away.

They had made it before the altar in the little church where her father had preached, all right, just not the way they'd planned. Althea remembered standing by his casket, saying her last goodbye. She hadn't had the chance to wear her mother's wedding gown. Instead, she'd put on the plain black dress she'd worn for both her parents' funerals.

Bill had been Althea's salt of the earth. She had a feeling Jared would be her spice. Gently she rubbed her finger across one nipple and felt it tighten beneath her touch. If she knew how, she'd ease the tension that drew her insides as tight as a fiddler's bowstring.

She would learn. If only because he'd be checking on the progress she was making on his quilt, Jared would come back. If she had to, she'd seduce him.

Never again was Althea going to put off pleasure or wait for some nebulous time in the future the fates might snatch away before it could come to fruition.

FIVE

The next morning Trina's truck was already in the parking lot when Althea came out of her cabin. She forced a sleepy smile, waved while crossing the parking lot to the porch of the shop. "Morning," she yelled as she fit her key in the lock on the front door.

"You must've had a real good time over at the festival." Trina raked Althea with a knowing gaze, from the top of her tousled head to feet she'd shoved into the first pair of sandals she'd found.

Althea smiled. "We did. Did your boys blow off those firecrackers you said they brought home from South Carolina?"

"They sure did. You'd have thought they were shootin' off dynamite, all the noise they were making. Me, I'd rather have gone and watched the fireworks show over in Dahlonega. Here, I saved us a piece of jam cake. Want me to make the coffee to go with it?"

"Go ahead. I want to see how far you got the other day piecing Jared's quilt."

The older woman grinned. "Anxious to start quiltin' it for him after spending the day together, are you?"

"We had fun."

"Did he put the top down on that fancy car of his?"

"Uh-huh. The wind felt good." Not as good as his hard, lean body had felt, pressed against her from shoulder to thigh. Nor as sweet as the clean male taste of him on her lips. Althea gave up counting quilt blocks and set them back on the worktable. "You know how many blocks you made the other day?"

"Thirty-two. Ought to finish the rest this morning. Then I can sew them together. Have you got the pieces for the border cut out?"

"They're in the drawer." Althea took a slice of cake and set it on the tray beside her quilting stand. If not too many customers came in, she should finish the crib quilt today. She took a bite of the tangy-sweet cake, then looked over at Trina. "This is delicious."

"It's my boys' favorite. You know, my little Joe was askin' about you yesterday. Said he might be comin' courting you when he gets back from Chattanooga next month."

That was the last thing Althea wanted. Lanky, slow-talking Joe Wells hadn't appealed to her when they were kids, and he didn't make her heart beat any faster now. Besides, she imagined he was the serious kind who'd start thinking marriage before he'd even consider having any fun.

"Well, Trina, I'm sort of dating Jared now," she murmured. Smiling, she finished her cake, then started quilting around the last appliqué on the little quilt.

"I thought so." Trina grinned as she aligned the edges of two triangles, snapped the presser foot down on them, and set the sewing machine to humming.

Warning off the local boys was an advantage of going out with Jared that Althea hadn't thought of before. Trina wasn't the only well-meaning neighbor who'd tried to set her up with a son or brother since Bill's death. Althea grinned. Who could intimidate would-be suitors better than a man who'd made it big enough to buy himself an entire mountain?

When the first customers came in, she got up and showed two Floridā ladies her quilts. She rang up a four-figure sale when one of them decided she had to have a flashy Lone Star quilt for her son's bed at home. A steady stream of customers kept Althea getting up every few minutes, but she managed to get some quilting done despite the interruptions.

By noon, Trina finished the blocks and set them out on the worktable in the order Althea had sketched. A little later, Althea put the last stitch into the crib quilt. She'd drop it off at Jim and Mary's place tonight after she closed the shop. Maybe if Trina finished piecing it today, she'd take Jared's quilt top, too. She could stop by his place to show it to him.

"Hear Jared Cain took you to the festival over in Helen," Jim said when Althea climbed the four stairs to his front porch.

She smiled. "News travels fast. Where's Mary?"

"Inside with Gracie. She tripped over a rock over there, banged up her knee." He gestured toward the path that led to an old well, then at the package in Althea's hand. "What's that?"

"A present for your baby boy." The oak-slat rocker she sat down on reminded Althea of another porch, one where she could hear the rushing water and smell new wood mingled with the pungent fragrance from a massive cedar tree overhead. "Thanks for sending Jared my way. I'm making a quilt for him. Trina finished piecing the top today."

"Thought you could use the business." Jim met her gaze, then turned back to the block of wood he'd been whittling when she arrived. A man of few words, her brother.

"Althea! Tell me all about our mystery man." Mary was as bubbly as Jim was taciturn. With three-year-old Gracie on her hip, she waddled over, sat down beside Althea. "You know Jim won't put two words together if he can help it."

Jim looked up from his carving, smiled at his wife. "Cain's no different from you and me, sugar. Want me to take Gracie?"

"She's okay. I don't see Jim Simmons riding around the countryside in a two-seater convertible, making grown women stop and stare when he walks into a store."

"Those women are greedy. Know Jared's got big money," Jim grumbled. "The man puts on his pants same as any other man."

Mary shook her head, gave her husband a disgusted look. "Come on, Althea, tell me. What's Jared really like?"

A friendly hound thrust his head in Althea's lap. "Go on, boy," she said. The hound's ear felt as soft as velvet when she scratched it. "He's fun to be with. Easy to talk to."

"Don't forget handsome as sin," Mary said, her eyes twinkling in a face Althea thought seemed a little bloated, a lot red.

"Are you okay?"

Mary shifted Gracie on her lap. "I will be, soon as

this baby gets here. Doc says I've put on way too much weight."

That reminded Althea why she'd come over. "Here. I finished the baby's quilt today." She put the package on the table next to Mary's chair. "Hope you'll like it."

"I'm sure it's beautiful. But you didn't have to—"

"Hush. I wanted to make my nephew something."

They chatted a while longer, until Althea sensed Mary was getting tired. When she got up to go, Jim followed her to her car. "Is that Cain's quilt?" he asked when he looked on the passenger seat and saw the folded quilt top.

"The top for it." Althea reached over and lifted a corner of the material. "Trina finished piecing it this afternoon."

"Did you have fun at the festival?"

"Lots. We went tubing, did some sightseeing. Jared's a nice man." More than nice, Althea thought. He was downright sexy.

"You going home now to start quiltin'?"

"I'm going to see Jared first. I want to show it to him, make sure it's put together the way he wants it."

Jim frowned. "You be careful, goin' by yourself to that man's fancy place. I don't want my little sister getting hurt. Don't know how well ol' Jared would take to bein' prodded with a shotgun. He's been away from these hills a long time."

Twelve years her senior, Jim had been looking out for Althea ever since their folks had died. She sighed. "Jim, I'm not looking for a husband, just some fun. I can take care of myself."

"If you say so. Remember, Cain's just a few years

younger than me. He's probably used to fast city women. Watch out for yourself." His brow furrowed, Jim straightened up and met Althea's gaze. "I better get back to Mary. I'm worried about her." Then he strode away.

Althea was worried, too, but anticipation nudged her concern to the back of her mind as she headed for Big Bear Mountain. The sun had disappeared beyond the horizon when she pulled up in front of Jared's place. A cool breeze ruffled her hair. It made her shiver as she came onto the porch and lifted the door knocker.

At first Jared thought it was the wind. Then he heard the noise again, more insistent this time. Setting down his pen, he got up, jogged downstairs, and answered the door.

Althea.

"Come on in." Had he conjured her up in his mind? She seemed real enough, standing there with a limp-looking quilt draped over one arm.

Her smile warmed him, and her sweet scent filled the foyer when she stepped inside. Jared itched to touch her. Was she as soft all over as she was in the places where his fingers had already explored?

"I brought the quilt top for you to see," she said.

Her smile nearly took his breath away, and her soft drawl reminded him of summer nights like this one. Nights and beds, and naked flesh draped with patchwork the colors of the forest.

"Come on in. Let's see how it looks on the bed." Desire slammed into him. He clenched his fists, forced himself to keep his hands off her. They were still hardly more than strangers, he reminded himself.

Althea went upstairs ahead of him, her movements as graceful as the curved staircase. He followed, mesmerized. She smoothed the tangled covers where he'd dreamed last night, then spread the quilt top across his bed. When she stepped back, they collided.

No force on earth could have kept Jared from reaching out, encircling Althea's slender waist, and drawing her soft curves into the hard angles of his body. He buried his face in her hair as he drank in the smell of sweet flowers and sweeter woman. Sliding his hands along her soft, flat belly, then higher, he cupped her breasts, then teased her nipples into rock-hard pebbles through the layers of her clothes.

"Jared."

On her lips, his name sounded like a prayer. "You like this?" He brushed his thumbs across her nipples, a little harder than before. Then he bent his head and blew on the shell of her ear.

She sighed, wiggled her tight little backside against his already rigid flesh. He wanted to strip off his clothes and hers, toss her across the bed, and bury himself inside her until he couldn't tell where he ended and she began.

"Althea?"

She turned and framed his face with trembling fingers. "Take me to bed."

When he met her gaze, he saw desire and something else. Fear? His body screamed for him to give her what she said she wanted, but his mind urged caution.

"You're sure?"

She nodded, feeble confirmation but enough for a

mind dulled by passion. With eager fingers, he began slipping the small white buttons of her blouse from the loops that held them closed.

In slow motion, Althea reached down to tug the blouse loose from her skirt, but Jared clasped her shoulders. He tumbled both of them onto his bed. His hands scorched her back when he grappled with her bra, and his clean male scent nearly overwhelmed her.

The sensations were so intense, it took a burst of cool air to remind her she was naked to the waist. The taste of him on her lips, the delicious friction of his callused fingers at the waistband of her skirt, even the ragged sound of his breathing seemed magnified a thousand times.

Suddenly shy, she trembled. It was all she could do to keep her hands still. She had to force herself not to cross her arms in front of her to hide her breasts from his hot, hard gaze.

He touched her cheek, his expression concerned. "We don't have to do this."

"I want to."

"Good." Jared didn't know where he would have found the willpower to stop. Although no one had ever died of unrequited lust, he figured he might easily have become the first.

She licked her lips. Watching her watch him undress made him crazy. Suddenly clumsy, he fumbled with his zipper. When he hooked his thumbs into the waistbands of his jeans and briefs, shoved them down and kicked them onto the floor, he noticed the hungry look in her eyes. It nearly made him explode on the spot.

"You're awfully big."

He wasn't going to last long, not with her staring at him like that. "That's what you do to me."

He took her hand and brought it to his sex. As much as he needed to have her under him, surrounding him, he made himself lie still. While she explored him with gentle fingers, he rolled her nipples softly between his thumbs and forefingers.

Curiosity. Delight. Desire. He read the changing emotions on her face, was touched by her wonder, her innocence. With difficulty, he clamped down his own urgency. She'd probably had very few lovers, maybe no one except the boy who had died. "Easy, sweetheart," he murmured, capturing her hands and bringing them to his lips.

"Love me."

He wanted to, but he wanted to make it good for her. Marcie's complaints rang in his ears, made him doubt. Suddenly he felt inept, as if he were traveling this path for the first time. He pulled Althea into his arms, tugged up the covers. "Let's slow this down, sweetheart. Relax. We've got all night."

Then the phone rang.

SIX

"Damn."

"You'd better answer it." Althea stretched out across the bed next to Jared, picked up the phone, and handed it to him.

Scowling, he growled his name. Then his expression turned pensive. "It's for you. Your brother."

Why would Jim be calling her here? Althea pulled the sheet up higher, although she realized the idea that her brother could see her made no sense. "Hello."

The news wasn't good, and Jim sounded frantic. Mary had collapsed not long after Althea had left their house. They were at the hospital in Dahlonega, waiting for the helicopter that would rush Mary to a big hospital in Atlanta.

"I'll come right away." Jim had been there for her when she needed him. She'd be there for him now.

"What's wrong?" Jared was already up, pulling on his clothes, by the time Althea could crawl out of bed.

She had trouble finding her voice. "Jim's wife. The baby. Something's terribly wrong. They're taking her to Atlanta. I've got to go."

What if Mary died? How would Jim go on? What would happen to Gracie?

Jared cupped Althea's face between his callused palms. "Is someone taking care of their little girl?" he asked.

His concern touched Althea. "Mary's sister has her. I've got to get dressed and go." Suddenly aware of her near nudity, she crossed her arms across her breasts.

"They'll all be okay. Calm down, honey. I'll drive you."

The way Jared jumped right in, took charge of the situation startled her. "I can—"

"You've got no business going by yourself."

Maybe he was right. She took a deep breath, but that didn't do much toward calming her speeding pulse.

She couldn't help remembering another trip to another hospital. She'd never forget that night when Jim had stayed by her, never forget the pain of her own nails digging into her palms as she prayed in vain that Bill wouldn't die. Not able to speak, she nodded as she took the bra and blouse Jared pressed into her hands and put them on.

She followed him downstairs and let him settle her in his car. After he started the engine, he turned to her. "Where are we going?"

"University Hospital in Atlanta." How could she have failed to realize, when she noticed Mary's swollen ankles and unnaturally flushed cheeks this afternoon, that something was seriously wrong? "God, let Mary be all right."

Tires crunching gravel, Jared maneuvered around her Pathfinder, down Big Bear Mountain, and onto the highway. "She will be. You need to stop by your place?"

"No. Please hurry."

"Try to relax, Althea. I'll get you there, as fast as I can and still be sure we'll make it in one piece." As gently as he'd touched her moments earlier, Jared massaged the back of her hand with his thumb after he'd put the Mercedes through its gears. A full moon lit the way as they sped around mountains with treacherous hairpin curves. As grateful as she was for Jared's skill at handling the sports car, Althea was glad when they got to the interstate.

"You need some coffee?" he asked when he pulled off the highway at an all-night truck stop.

His voice warmed the dark cocoon of the car interior, made her smile despite her fear for Mary and Jim. "I'll get it while you pump the gas."

The drone of a hundred or more idling diesel engines and snippets of conversations transmitted over a dozen squawking CB radios hummed in Althea's ears long after they were back on the road, and it took almost as long for the acrid smell of gasoline to fade from her head. She sipped her coffee, glad for the quiet comfort that surrounded them in the car as they sped down Interstate 75.

Jared reached over, gently pried her clenched fingers loose. "Relax, sweetheart. We'll be there soon."

"It's just—I don't know. I'm so afraid—"

"You can call the hospital." He reached for the car phone, but she stilled his hand.

"They'd never be able to track down Jim and Mary. Not in that huge place."

He held onto her hand, soothed her with his touch. Althea leaned against the headrest, watched him drive. Through half-closed eyelids, she studied his reassuring profile—backlit in the surreal glow from lights of cars and trucks they passed, silhouetted in the darkness relieved only by the reflection from the car's control panel when they had the highway to themselves.

Lights came more often now as they neared Atlanta. Her mind focused on why they were here, speeding through the night to—*God, please let Mary and the baby be all right.*

Althea couldn't keep her muscles from clenching with fear, but having Jared there with her made the tension easier to bear. His quiet confidence bolstered her spirits, and his presence reassured her. Although the thought crossed her mind that she was getting in too deep, she was glad she'd accepted his help, because she doubted she could have born the waiting without him.

A few minutes later, Jared watched Althea run into her brother's arms as soon as they stepped off the elevator onto the hospital's maternity floor.

He held back so she and Jim could have a minute alone. The man looked ashen beneath his leathery tan, and his shoulders drooped as though he'd aged years in the week or so since he delivered Jared's handmade dining table and chairs. Jim had to be going through hell.

When Jared noticed Althea's hands were shaking, he moved closer and put a hand on her shoulder. He heard Jim say his baby boy had been born and that they'd just taken his wife to Intensive Care.

"Mary will be all right, won't she?" Althea asked.

Jim shook his head. "We've got to wait and see. The doctors say she had a stroke. She quit breathing twice on the way down here." He paused, then continued, his voice so low Jared figured he must have been talking to himself. "I should never have touched her again, not after the hard time she had with Gracie."

"The baby?" Jared was almost afraid to ask. When he saw Jim's stricken look, he wished he'd kept his mouth shut.

Jim turned away, then stared silently out the window. Althea took Jared's hand. "The baby's here almost six weeks early, but the doctors say he's going to be okay," she told him. "Jim's so concerned about Mary right now, he's having a hard time thinking about his son."

For several tense hours they sat, pretending to sip the vile stuff that passed for coffee. Jared kept buying soggy cups of it from a machine in the corner of the waiting room.

Jim paced the length of the hall, then stopped to stare through the glass in the swinging doors marked ICU. He came back and sat down for a few minutes, then repeated his trek. Every hour he'd disappear through those doors to spend the five minutes the nurses would allow him with his wife. By morning, he looked ready to be admitted himself.

Jared had never felt so helpless. Or so mixed up. One minute, he longed to care for somebody as much as Jim obviously loved his wife. As much as Althea cared about them both. With his next breath, he thanked God for sparing him the kind of anguish Althea and her brother were suffering.

Helpless to do more, Jared held Althea's hand and murmured hopeful platitudes. When she finally nodded off to sleep, he tucked a pillow behind her head.

The sun was streaming into the solitary window in

the waiting room by the time Jim came out of the ICU again, a tired smile on his face. He told Jared Mary had come to and that the doctors held out hope now that she'd recover from her ordeal.

"You're welcome to go rest at my place," Jared told Jim, who looked as though he might fall over any minute. "It's less than a half hour from here."

Jim shook his head. "Thanks, but I don't want to leave. Mary will need me here when she wakes up, and the nurse said they'd let me hold the baby soon. You go on. Take Althea with you." He looked over, shook his head at the sight of her, sound asleep sitting up. "She's going to get a crick in her neck, sleepin' in the chair like that."

Jared smiled. Had it been only eight hours since Althea had showed up on his doorstep and said she wanted to make love? So much had happened, it seemed hardly possible. "Yes, she is," he replied when Jim gave him a peculiar look.

"Don't you go hurting my sister. She's been through a lot."

It felt strange, knowing he'd have to answer to someone else beside his own conscience if things didn't work out for Althea the way she wanted. Jared decided he didn't mind the feeling. He held out his hand to Jim as he met the other man's weary gaze. "Hurting her's the last thing on my mind. Althea's special."

"That she is."

Jared gave Jim the phone number at his condo and for his cell phone. "I know Althea will want to know right away when she'll be able to see Mary and her nephew," he said before gently waking her.

* * *

At the condo, he peeled away Althea's clothes. God, but she was sexy, all sleepy-eyed and warm. He reminded himself she had to be exhausted, more in need of sleep than sex.

"Lie down with me." Her eyelids drooped, but she smiled and held out her arms.

No force on earth could have kept Jared from stretching out beside her. He pulled her close and shuddered when his body reacted as if it he hadn't just denied it a good night's sleep.

Good thing he hadn't undressed, he thought, even though his jeans were getting tighter by the minute. Jared reminded himself Althea needed rest. Until he was certain she'd fallen asleep, he held her. Then he got up. He'd never been able to sleep once the sun came up, and with Althea beside him in bed, sleeping was the last thing on his mind.

The condo Jared had called home for nearly ten years looked bleak. It seemed as if no one had ever lived within its sand-colored, sand-textured walls or sunk their bare feet into plush carpeting a few shades lighter than the walls. The brown leather sofa and chairs, dark wood tables and desks—even the bevel-edged mirrors on the wall—had all the personality of an expensive hotel suite.

He wondered how he'd lived here, worked at the computer in the corner of the living room for hours at the time, even days on end, yet not noticed before that the place had no heart, nothing to indicate a real human being had ever been in residence.

He'd known something was missing from his life.

That's why he'd bought the mountain where he was born, had a house built there. Still, Jared had the sinking feeling that place would have ended up as sterile as this one if it hadn't been for his chance discovery of the quilt square. The ragged piece of cloth that had led him to Althea.

With Althea, he saw light and color and texture. Saw her as woman, himself as . . . certainly not the robot Marcie had compared him to. Robots reacted according to a programmer's whim, a designer's control. When he was with Althea, his emotions grabbed him, made him react unpredictably. She made him think with his heart and not his mind. As if he were a living, breathing man.

Hell, he was a man, if his body's reactions to her were any indication.

He looked at one of the mirrors, tried to recall some of the times he and Marcie had shared here. There were pitifully few in his memory bank. Although he had no trouble remembering many hours they'd spent together in his office or hers, going over some marketing scheme she'd devised, the picture of her here wouldn't come clear.

Business partners. They'd been more that than lovers, though they'd spent hundreds of nights here or at her place, locked in each other's arms. When they decided to call it quits, neither of them had needed more than one small box to haul away the personal belongings they'd left in one another's respective spaces.

When he'd been with Marcie, he hadn't felt out of place here. Now Jared stared at his reflection. Why did the condo strike him now as cold when he'd never given the place a thought before, except to consider it convenient to hole up in when he had to leave his office?

Had Marcie been right? Had he really been a cold son-of-a-bitch, a robot who went through the motions of being a man? Jared shook his head, looked away. What he saw in the mirror disturbed him. Would he tire of Althea and lose interest in Big Bear Mountain? Would he revert to being the mechanical creature Marcie used to accuse of having built a business empire at the cost of his own self?

Jared couldn't figure out answers now. He needed caffeine. In the kitchen he found the essentials and brewed a pot of coffee. Damn, but the stuff tasted bitter. *Medicine,* he told himself as he slugged down a mug full of muddy liquid that was almost as bad as what he'd bought from the machine at the hospital.

The clock over the sink said ten o'clock. Since he was here, he'd take care of a little business. Settling down at the kitchen table, he picked up the phone and called his assistant, Laura Peters.

While he and Laura ironed out some details about the holiday ad campaign, Jared couldn't stop himself from thinking about Althea. They'd practically flown from Big Bear Mountain to Atlanta. There hadn't been time to grab more clothes than what they'd tugged back onto their bodies after Jim's call.

He had extra things here, but Althea would need clean clothes. Before he hung up, Jared asked Laura to arrange for a store to send over something for Althea to wear.

* * *

Althea blinked, then closed her eyes against brilliant streaks of light that filtered through vertical blinds into an unfamiliar room.

Slowly it came back to her. Mary's stroke. The baby. Jim looking as though he'd lost his world. Hope had mingled with fear on his face after his last visit to the ICU before she left with Jared.

Oh, no. Jared. They'd been about to make love when Jim had called.

She opened her eyes again, looked around, then stretched out across the large, firm mattress. Jared had brought her here to his condo. She remembered he'd lain down beside her. His warmth, the strength evident in his muscular arms, had lulled her back to sleep. Where was he now?

Soft music filled the air. Althea wanted to curl up, bury her head in a soft, fat pillow, and close her eyes again. The faint scent of tangy aftershave that lingered on the pillowcase reminded her of Jared and the way he'd skimmed her naked body with gentle callused fingers. His touch had evoked a sense of peace, safety.

She recognized his voice, low and sexy, singing along with the soft country song. He sounded a bit off-key, and his words were muffled by solid walls and distance.

She stretched, then smiled. Jared Cain was more than a hard body and an arresting face. He was a genuinely decent man. Not only did she want him, she liked him—and that scared Althea half to death.

Suddenly wide awake, she sat up. What was she doing, mooning over Jared when Mary might be dead or dying? She grabbed the phone on the nightstand. While she waited for directory assistance to find the hospital's phone number, Jared strode into the room, still wet and naked except for a beige towel he'd knotted around his narrow waist. He set a good-sized bag on the chair beside her wrinkled blouse and skirt.

"Jim called about an hour ago, told me to let you sleep. His wife's going to be all right." Taking the receiver from Althea's hand as he sat beside her on the bed, Jared set it on its base. "Want to drive over and see her, make sure Jim doesn't need anything?"

"Uh-huh." Relief washed over her. She wouldn't wish the tearing grief she'd felt the day Bill died on anyone, much less her brother. "You should have waked me earlier," she said when he bent and brushed his lips softly across her cheek.

"You needed the rest."

"So did you."

He shrugged. "I can't go to sleep when it's light out. I'll be okay. This isn't the first time I've stayed up all night. Probably won't be the last."

He was obviously tired. Dark circles accentuated his eyes, reminded her he'd set aside whatever plans he might have had to bring her here, to stand by her and lend her his considerable strength. Every new facet she uncovered made her like him more. Not only was Jared the sexiest man Althea had ever seen, he was the kind of man she could easily fall in love with—if she hadn't sworn never to risk her heart again.

She got up and forced herself to ignore the enticing picture Jared presented. His dark hair was damp from the shower, and nothing but a skimpy towel hid his hard, fit body from her gaze. Suddenly shy, Althea wrapped the beige top sheet, togalike, around her naked body.

"Shower?"

SEVEN

The word sounded incredibly intimate, spoken in that deep, mesmerizing voice. "With you?"

"Not if we're going to get over to see your brother and his wife anytime soon. Besides, I just took mine a few minutes ago. May I have a rain check?"

Jared stood, shook his head, and shot Althea a wry smile. "Bathroom's through that door. You'll find towels, soap, shampoo—most everything you might need, I guess—in the linen closet. There ought to be something that will fit you in that bag."

He motioned toward a large sack that bore the name and logo of what looked like a pricey Atlanta boutique, then opened a door and stepped inside a walk-in closet. "I'll grab myself some clean clothes and get out of your way."

"You went shopping?" she asked, confused.

"I had my assistant make a phone call. The store sent over some things for you." Jared stepped out of the closet and grinned over the khaki pants and short-sleeve polo shirt he held chest-high. "I thought you might want something clean to wear, and there's nothing I have that would even halfway fit you. Hope something in there will do."

His thoughtfulness apparently knew no bounds. "Jared, you shouldn't have. Thank you, though. How did you know what size I am?"

"I described you to Laura. She took it from there, and said she'd tell the store to send some things where the fit wasn't all that important."

Althea liked the pair of bright blue shorts and a sleeveless white top with a stylized blue-and-yellow flower appliqué she'd like to duplicate and use for a quilting project. Taking a deep breath, she checked out the price tags. "Oh, God."

"What's wrong?"

Althea's budget didn't allow for shopping sprees at designer boutiques. She worried her lower lip between her teeth, aware she was doing it but not able to quit. "Jared, I can't afford clothes like these." Over a hundred-fifty dollars for a pair of shorts and a top seemed obscene. Althea could have made them out of comparable fabrics for less than twenty dollars. "I'll just put my own things back on. They're not that dirty."

"Consider them presents. I don't expect you to pay for something I ordered." Jared shrugged, then pointed toward the bathroom. "Go on, now. Get showered and dressed so we can go see your new nephew."

Althea was tempted to say okay. Whoever selected the clothes had chosen three outfits she'd have probably picked out for herself, had money not been a concern.

One, a loose-fitting, dark purple dress with hand embroidery decorating the square neckline and hem, made her drool. The other, white cotton slacks and a T-shirt whose red and navy blue design gave it a nautical look, reminded her of what well-dressed city women wore when they came shopping up in the mountains.

If she kept them, though, she'd never be able to repay Jared. "I can't accept these things. They're—too much."

"For heaven's sake, Althea, it's only a few clothes." His brow creased, as if he found her reticence annoying.

The ring Bill had given her when he'd asked her to be his wife had cost less than these three outfits, but it had meant so much. In her world and Bill's, six hundred dollars was a fortune. In Jared's, it apparently amounted to pocket change. She'd take the clothes, and try to accept them as casually as he seemed to think she should.

"All right. I'll feel better, knowing my clothes aren't tired, even if I am."

Jared grinned. "That's better. I'll wait for you in the living room."

His apartment boasted every imaginable luxury, yet it told her nothing about Jared. Thick beige towels blotted away water with grim efficiency but lent not one whit of color to a spacious bathroom done in toast and beige.

After she put on the purple dress, Althea smoothed a woven beige coverlet over the bed. If there were any meaning to the framed picture of black circles and tan triangles that hung above a headboard made of plain oak slats, she couldn't discern it. Even the floor, lush as it felt under her feet, wore an impersonal cloak of thick beige carpet.

She gathered her things and headed down a narrow hallway toward the sound of music. There Jared was, hunched over a computer, looking at some kind of report on the screen.

Maybe she was wrong. Maybe this place did reflect something about its owner. Emptiness. Lack of emotion.

Or was it loneliness? Had Jared Cain focused all of himself on his business because he'd lost family? Friends? A lover?

This place bore no evidence Jared had ever had anyone to care about. Not a photo to be seen, nor some incongruous piece of furniture scarred by people's living. Not even one memento stood out to hint it might have once triggered an emotional response from him. Althea had thought his beautiful mountain home sparsely furnished, but this condo made the cabin seem homelike by comparison.

How could a man who had so much live in such a sterile place? She thought of her own small cabin, where she used every available surface to celebrate her memories. Photos in mismatched frames, her great-grandma's blue willow teapot, crocheted doilies her aunt had made when Althea was a little girl. The portrait of Bill in his uniform, on the table by her bed in the same place she'd put it when he'd given it to her a week before he died.

Jared would probably think her home impossibly cluttered, her memories trite. But maybe not. He'd been insistent that he have a quilt made exactly the way his mother had made that square he'd brought to her shop.

Maybe his homes seemed sterile because he had no tangible evidence of the experiences that had made him the man he was. He seemed to be searching for something, though. Whether it was for himself or for a past to give meaning to his present, she didn't know.

"I'm ready," Althea said, and she couldn't help noticing how his expression turned from brooding to animated when he looked up at her. She could tell he wanted her, probably as much as she yearned for him. That much was clear.

"Let's go then." As if he couldn't get away quickly enough, Jared turned off the computer and ushered Althea out the door.

When they walked into Mary's hospital room, Jim twitched, then opened his eyes. He looked as though he'd been through World War III, but he got up and hugged Althea. Then he shook Jared's hand.

"How is she, Jim?" Althea asked, her voice little more than a whisper as she looked at the pale woman sleeping on the bed.

"All right. Doc said she has to take off a bunch of that extra weight she gained. Damn, Althea, I don't know what I'd have done if I lost her."

Jared never wanted to feel the kind of anguish he sensed in Jim's ragged voice. Maybe Marcie's assessment of him was right. Perhaps he didn't have the capacity for such deep emotional commitment, and just maybe that lack was not all bad after all.

"Thanks for bringing Althea," Jim said when he finally released her and turned to Jared. "Y'all going home tonight?"

Jared didn't know. "Althea?"

"What?"

"Do you want to drive back tonight or shall we stay here? Makes no difference to me." It did, though. Jared wanted to make love with Althea, and he didn't want their first time together to be in the bed he'd sometimes shared with Marcie. He wanted them to go to Big Bear Mountain. Go home.

She hesitated, turned to Jim. "What about Gracie?"

"Mary's sister said she'd keep her until I bring Mary and the baby home."

"Jared, I think we should stay here tonight. I hate for you to drive without having any sleep. I'll need to open the shop on Thursday, though. I don't have anyone scheduled to work with me then, and I can't very well not open up. Summer's no time to be missing out on tourist business."

Jared tried to hide his disappointment. "All right. I could stand to get a little more work done while we're in Atlanta. Jim, how long will Mary and the baby have to stay here?"

Jim shrugged. "A week or so, I guess. Until they can get her blood pressure to stay down."

"Can we see the baby?" Althea asked.

"Sure. The baby doctor says he'll be out of the incubator in another day or two. He could probably do without it now, but they don't want to take any chances." A grin lit Jim's craggy face, so much it nearly wiped away the look of exhaustion from his features. "You know, that little guy weighed over seven pounds?"

Jared couldn't recall having heard Jim put so many words together in one sentence before. He could practically feel the other man's pride and love when he spoke as they walked down the hall to the neonatal ICU. When they stood in front of a glass window and looked down at a red, screaming, incredibly tiny infant encased in a clear plastic bubble, Jared wished briefly for his own shot at immortality.

He glanced at Althea. Her features took on a special

softness, almost a glow, as she stared at her brand-new nephew. How might a child of theirs look?

Taken aback at the unexpected direction his thoughts were taking, he turned to Jim. "If I'm going to get any work done today, we need to get going. You're welcome to come over, stay at my place while you're in Atlanta."

"Thanks anyway, but I'll stay right here, close to Mary and this little guy. Althea can tell you, I don't have much trouble sleeping anywhere."

She laughed. "That's right. He'll sleep just fine in that big chair by Mary's bed. Jim, you take good care of this little fellow. What's his name, by the way?"

"Jim, Junior."

"Figures." Playfully, she shook her head, then stood on tiptoe to brush her lips across her brother's leathery cheek. "Jared, I'm ready if you are."

Apparently Jared had meant it when he said he had to work. Not sleepy after the long nap she'd taken earlier in the day, Althea roamed around his condo while he talked on the phone. He frowned occasionally as he looked at reports and charts on a computer screen.

Maybe she'd fix them something to eat. His kitchen was a technological marvel, the likes of which she hadn't seen since her home-ec classes in college. When she opened the cabinets, though, she saw they might as well be empty. A couple of cans of chili, some microwave popcorn, and half a box of saltine crackers. The crackers had to be stale, she imagined, since they'd been open at least as long as Jared had been at his place on Big Bear Mountain. Almost a month.

The side-by-side refrigerator boasted nothing but an

overflowed automatic icemaker, two Bud longnecks, and a half-empty jar of yellow mustard. Disappointed, she closed it. "He might as well not have a kitchen," she muttered.

"Huh?"

She turned, looked up at Jared, hoped her cheeks weren't as flushed as they felt. "Do you always sneak up on folks?"

"It's fun sometimes." He shot her a grin that took her breath away. "What were you grumbling about?"

"You don't eat here very much, do you?"

He shrugged. "When I'm here, I usually have some cereal and milk."

"Like I said, you don't eat here very much. I was going to fix us something to eat."

He rested his hands on her shoulders, then bent to brush his lips across hers. "I'll take you out—or we can have something delivered. I didn't bring you here to slave over a hot stove."

Althea looked up at Jared and smiled. "I didn't mean to disturb your work."

"You didn't. I'm waiting for a new game to download so I can check it out."

"Must be nice to make your living playing kids' games on a computer."

"Yeah?"

"Yeah." It was fun to tease Jared, watch the tiny lines at the corners of his mouth and eyes deepen as though he wanted to laugh.

His expression turned serious. "Sometimes I wish that were all there was to running Cain Software. There's less play, more hard work, every time we introduce a new software package. I should have gotten a degree in business, not computer science."

"But you love it. No one could get so immersed in anything they didn't care about."

Jared shrugged, but his expression confirmed her suspicion that he really didn't mind that he had to manage what he'd developed into a successful business.

"You seem to have done right well for yourself." That was an understatement.

His hands tightened on her shoulders before he let her go. "I guess I'm doing okay for a poor boy from Big Bear Mountain. Do you like Italian?" he asked as he dug through a stack of papers he took from a drawer.

Althea pictured a spicy pizza, dripping with cheese. "Love it."

"Pizza or pasta?"

"Pizza."

He handed her two dog-eared menus. "If you're hungry now, we'd better order from Sal's. Roman Palace makes the best pizza in Atlanta, but they'll take anywhere from an hour to an hour and a half to get it here."

Althea could wait. After they'd ordered the Roman Palace's special, a tossed salad, and a six-pack of soft drinks, she coaxed Jared into going back to the game he'd wanted to test.

She stared at the four stark walls and wished she'd brought along some quilting to keep her occupied. Once in a while she glanced at Jared and the jewel-toned action figures on the screen of his computer.

When he looked up, his face broke out into that smile she couldn't resist. "Come on over and watch.

Laura thinks this game's going to make Cain Software another million or two. Tell me what you think."

After watching for a few minutes, Althea found her head was starting to spin. Playing action games on the computer wasn't her idea of relaxing. "Kids will love it," she said, and she was certain they would.

Jared switched to another screen. "Look. Which one of these packages would you pick up first if you were looking for a present for your niece?"

One box featured a full-body shot of a red-clad actor who apparently represented the hero of the game. On the other box was a blowup of his face, complete with a fearsome scowl. "White Lightning," the name of the game, stood out on both boxes—one white on a neon green lightning bolt, the other in black-bordered white letters on a red bolt. Action figures like the ones Althea had seen on the screen were pictured on the left corner of each box, above the Cain Software logo.

"The one with the actor's face," Althea told him, although she doubted she'd ever pick such a gift for her three-year-old niece even if Gracie had access to a computer.

"Why?"

She had no idea. During the next half-hour, until their pizza arrived, Jared picked her brain about her reactions to the proposed packaging for this new game. She felt more than a twinge of jealousy when she learned that Marcie, his former fiancée, had been an expert at the art of marketing his products. It was obvious that he missed her on a professional if not a personal level.

When bedtime came, Althea found herself in his big bed, alone. For a long time she couldn't sleep, knowing as she did that Jared was in the living room, doing work that ostensibly couldn't wait another day.

The next morning when he woke her, he let her know he'd fallen asleep on the sofa while studying some financial projections.

"I need to go to my office to sign some papers. Want to see where I work?" he asked.

Somehow going where he worked and meeting his employees sounded too serious. As if they had something going that was more than good times. "I'd better go by the hospital. Mary sounded as though she'd like some company when I spoke to her."

Jared smiled. "I'll drop you off there."

When he pulled up in front of the hospital, he reached over and drew Althea into his arms. While she visited with Mary and Jim, the feel and taste of Jared stayed on her lips, and on her mind.

Althea had leaned on Jared these past two days. She'd taken comfort and affection from him, in a way she'd sworn she wouldn't do again that wet, dark morning they lowered Bill's casket into the ground. She'd shared her fears, let Jared calm them.

Worse, she wanted to comfort him, make him see and feel life in vivid hues, not the bland neutrals with which he'd surrounded himself. And she wanted to look into his heart, learn if the woman he'd nearly married still lived there.

She had to forget the emotions. Focus on the way Jared made her feel. Recall the rasp of his callused fingers against her tenderest flesh. Picture his eyes flashing emerald fire at the sight of her. Think about the smell of the woods and his cologne and him, mingled into an aphrodisiac potion like no other she'd ever known. Savor the way he'd felt, hard and lean and ready, weighing her down. Possessing her.

Would he ask her to stay with him tonight? Would they take up when they got back to his house where they'd left off after Jim's call?

As she watched Jared drive, Althea wished his talented hands were on her instead of the leather-covered steering wheel. Above all, she wished all she wanted was to satisfy the physical needs this man had awakened in her.

EIGHT

She looked like an angel in the loose purple dress. Jared wondered how he could ever have thought her plain. Unlike Marcie, Althea's beauty came from the inside out. She was different from any woman he'd ever known.

In the light of the full moon, she smiled slightly in her sleep. She'd looked disappointed when he'd sent her to bed alone last night. Would she stay with him now if he asked her to?

He drove up the winding road to his cabin. Instead of pulling into the garage, he parked next to her Pathfinder and shut off the car engine. Gently, he touched her face, then smoothed an errant strand of hair off her cheek. Her eyelids fluttered, then opened.

"We're back."

She smiled. "May I stay?"

"I was hoping you would." Jared got out of the car and walked around it. When he stopped, he stretched. Suddenly he realized he hadn't had more than a few hours' sleep for nearly three days. "I'd like to fall asleep in your arms," he said when he opened the passenger door. That was just about all he'd be able to do, at least until he got a few hours' rest.

Walking arm in arm with her, through moonlight-dappled darkness toward the floodlights that illuminated the porch, gave Jared an unfamiliar feeling. A feeling of coming home. Suddenly he realized how much he'd missed the sense of belonging he hadn't experienced for years—not since he'd lived with his parents farther up the side of this mountain.

He imagined the quilt Althea was making draped across his bed—their bed. What other feminine touches would she make that would make his house their home?

Where had that crazy thought come from? Jared tried to force it out of his head. Hadn't he proved with Marcie that he wasn't even passable husband material?

He reined in his imagination and chalked up his aberrant fantasy to exhaustion as he walked Althea up the stairs. "You take the bathroom first," he told her. Then he stared out the window at stars that had never before seemed so bright.

"I borrowed one of your shirts," she said when she came back.

Jared turned, met her gaze. "It never looked so good on me." The tail of his long-sleeved white dress shirt came nearly to her knees, drew his attention to her gorgeous legs. "Come here."

She met his gaze and smiled, then walked into his outstretched arms. Her warm breath tickled his chest, sent the blood slamming through his weary veins to pool between his legs. "Your turn for the shower," she said, her voice as suggestive as her words were mundane.

Maybe Jared wasn't as tired as he'd thought. His sex throbbed, his skin burned. He'd tuck her in bed, take a quick shower, and then . . .

When he crawled in bed beside her a few minutes later, he could see that she had fallen asleep. Just as well. He was feeling muscles he'd forgotten he had, aching from his temples to his toes. There was always tomorrow, he promised himself as he drew Althea into his arms and drifted off to sleep.

When he woke up, it was to her goodbye kiss. "Stay," he murmured, still more than half asleep but already hard and needy.

"I have to open the shop. Besides, I'd like to start quilting this." She picked up his quilt top, then shot him a sweet, sleepy smile. The bright design on her shirt made her eyes look impossibly blue. Matching shorts gave him an arousing view of long, shapely legs he couldn't help imagining wrapped tight around his hips when they made love.

If they ever did. Jared tamped down his desire, tried to smile. Not for the first time he reminded himself no one had ever died from sexual frustration. "Come back tonight?"

"I should work on your quilt if I'm going to get it done when I promised."

"Do it here." For some reason he couldn't put into words, it was important that Althea work on his quilt in this house. Her presence made the sterile rooms come alive and transformed this elaborate cabin into a home. The idea of watching her ply her needle here excited him. "Please."

She smiled. "You don't have a quilting frame."

"I'll buy one. You sell them, don't you?"

"Yes, but—"

He drew her down beside him and stroked the patchwork she held over her heart. "I'll set the frame up in front of the fireplace, and you can do your thing while I check out a new Cain Software game or two. Then if the fates are kind, we can come to bed. I'd like to continue where we left off the other night."

Smiling, Althea bent over and traced the seam of his lips with her tongue. "Sounds too good to pass up. I'll bring us some food. See you about six o'clock. Sweet dreams." She kissed him hard, then got up, hurried out the door. He listened to the fading sounds her feet made as she went down the circular stairs.

She'd slept in two strange beds, both Jared's, for three straight nights, and she was still a virgin. Some success she was as a seductress.

Althea drove down Big Bear Mountain, slowed to a crawl as she passed by the tiny church where her father had preached. The church she'd attended all her life. A glance at the graveyard reassured her the wreath she'd put on Bill's grave last month was still in place and that the plastic flowers in the urn between her parents' headstones hadn't faded in the sun.

Thank God there wouldn't be another funeral in the immediate future, another grave to tend. Mary and the baby would be all right. Althea frowned. Somehow she'd made it through this latest crisis without reliving too much of the pain she'd felt when Bill had died. She wondered why.

Then it hit her. She'd had Jared to lean on, to hold her hand until the crisis had passed. Jared had been her anchor.

When she pulled into the parking lot at her shop,

Althea closed her eyes. She tried to picture Bill, but she saw Jared's face instead.

She'd promised herself whatever might happen with Jared would be strictly physical. There would be no emotional commitment. No love. No emotion at all beyond wanting and mutual respect. When, Althea asked herself, had the enigmatic executive gotten under her skin?

Her vow to guard her heart, to concentrate totally on physical sensation and sexual fulfillment wasn't working, not anymore. How was she going to squelch the tender emotions he brought out in her by being a genuinely nice guy?

She didn't have a clue, other than to keep in mind the differences in their lifestyles, to remind herself of her resolve to keep it strictly physical each time she saw him. And to immerse herself in work. When she pulled up in front of her cabin, she fished out her keys, but went straight to the shop. She had to keep Jared Cain off her mind.

The way she did every day, Althea straightened stock and waited on customers. When Jared walked in around eleven o'clock, she was on the phone with Bea Elder, letting her know she'd finally sold the matching twin bed quilts the woman had placed on consignment more than a year earlier.

"Big sale?" he asked after she hung up.

"It was, for the lady who made the quilts. She's been calling nearly every day the last few months, wondering if any of my customers showed any interest."

Jared glanced down at the counter, then picked up a round fabric cutter. His expression sober, he appeared to give the tool a thorough inspection before meeting Althea's gaze. "I didn't know you did consignments."

"I don't. Not really. When somebody wants to sell their crafts, I put them in the store if I think they'll move. Bea's no artist, but she does pretty good hand-quilting—and she needs every little bit of money she can get. She's trying to raise her daughter's two kids on nothing but her social security checks."

"How would having this co-op you were telling me about help Bea any more than you help her by letting her sell her stuff here in the store?"

Althea handed Jared two quilted pillow tops. "Bea made the blue one. There's nothing really wrong with it, but . . ." She shrugged.

He studied both pieces, then met her gaze. "It's really not as attractive as the other one."

"You're right. In a co-op, women who make quilts to sell would split up the work based on who does what part of the process best. Bea, for instance, would do the hand-quilting on quilt tops someone else had made. She's good and fast at that, while other quilters are better designing, cutting, and piecing. Trina Wells, who pieced your quilt, is one of the best I've ever seen at that part of quilt-making, but she can't do the actual quilting at all well."

Jared smiled. "I see. The co-op could have sort of a small-scale assembly line, with everybody doing what they do best. I imagine Mom would have liked that sort of factory a lot better than the one she worked in after we moved to Atlanta."

"Where did she work?"

"At a company that made ceramic dishes. She

sprayed glaze on plates before they went into the kilns." A pained look crossed Jared's handsome face.

"Sounds as though working on craft projects would have been considerably more fun."

"I imagine. Mom came home exhausted every night, hacking and coughing from the smell of the glaze. I never heard her mention the word 'fun' in connection with her job."

The sadness that radiated from Jared sobered Althea. She had a sudden urge to hold him, hug away memories she was certain caused him pain. "I'm sure your mom was glad to have any job so she could take care of you."

"Yeah. I'm just sorry she didn't live long enough to benefit from my success."

Althea reached out, touched Jared's hand. "I'm sure she's looking down from heaven, proud as she can be of how her boy turned out."

"I hope so." He squeezed her fingers as he gave her a halfhearted smile. "What is it you want to do at your co-op, besides assembly-line production of quilts?"

"I plan to advertise for local women to bring in all kinds of things they've made on a consignment basis—everything from needlework to artwork to homemade jellies and cider. We'll package the crafts distinctively at the co-op, then sell them at wholesale to stores all over the country."

Althea looked at Jared. His intent expression encouraged her to go on. "Maybe we could eventually set up a retail store on the internet. The co-op could open up all sorts of doors for people who need help to stay in these mountains and make a decent living while holding onto their pride."

He nodded, but his brow creased as though he were doing some serious thinking. "Wouldn't putting a craft co-op practically next door to your store hurt your business?" he asked after a moment's pause.

Meeting his thoughtful gaze, she smiled. "I don't think so. My main business here is selling quilting supplies and fabric, not the finished quilts I've made, although I do sell a few. A couple from Chattanooga just bought Bea's twin bed quilts to give their twin grandsons for Christmas. They'd really wanted another set that I'd made, but Bea's were cheaper."

"Would they have bought yours if you hadn't had hers?"

"Probably not. They struck me as folks who'd set a budget and meant to keep to it."

Jared set the pillow tops down and strode across the room. "How much would it take to set this co-op up in business?"

Althea named a figure. "That would get it off the ground. At least it would have, eighteen months ago. Why?"

"Because I might be able to help."

"Why would you want to do that?" Might he be willing to share his knowledge about starting a business, maybe even give her some pointers as to how she might turn her dreams into reality?

"Maybe as a sort of tribute to my mom . . ." His voice trailed off, as though he were deep in thought. Then he grinned. "We can talk more about it later. How about pointing me in the direction of that frame you'll need if you're going to work on my quilt at my place?"

"To your left."

He glanced first at the boxed stands, then at the big

frame she had set up in the center of the store. "That's the one you usually use, isn't it?"

"When I'm here. If I'm working at home, I use a smaller one, a lot like that portable frame by your left foot."

"Why?"

"I don't have enough room in my cabin to set up a full-size frame."

"There's plenty of empty space in my living room." Jared strode over to the big frame and ran a finger across the smoothly sanded pine. "Do you have another one like this?"

"Up there."

His glanced at the top of a shelf where several disassembled frames were collecting dust. "How much talent does it take to put one of these things together?" he asked after dragging down a tied-together bunch of sanded wood pieces that bore more resemblance to a giant jigsaw puzzle than a quilting frame.

"A little effort, a screwdriver, and a hammer. I can—"

"I'll do it." Jared grinned, as if eager to meet the challenge offered by some smooth-sanded pine and a bag of hardware.

She tried to give him the frame, but he insisted on paying the full price she'd marked on them when she bought them from Jim last December. Call for the bulky frames was spotty, but Althea had seen her purchase as a way of helping Jim out, keeping his family from suffering while his business had been going through the slow winter months last year.

NINE

Jared set up the quilting frame, then glanced at his watch. One o'clock. Five more hours before Althea would be back. He could work or he could go outside and split more logs from a hickory tree that had blown over during a storm.

Neither option appealed. As he sipped hot coffee and watched the creek's crystalline water tumble over rocks on its journey to the valley, Jared imagined a craft co-op, no longer Althea's dream but a reality.

He could help her make it happen. It was too late to save his mother from years of drudgery, not to mention what had seemed like centuries of his uncle's grudging charity; but maybe a co-op would keep other families from having to leave the mountains to go places they weren't wanted, and where they didn't fit in.

Setting his empty cup on the counter, Jared grabbed his keys. An hour later, he was having lunch with his real estate agent at a little restaurant on the square in Blairsville, explaining what he had in mind.

"Althea's had her eye on this piece of property," Harriet Tucker said as she flipped through her listing book. "Here. It used to be a gas station, years ago. Then a flea market. Hasn't been used at all for five or ten years, I don't guess. But it's cheap."

Jared glanced from the photo of a shabby building to the facing page where asking price, acreage, and financing information were summarized. "That it is. Would the owner consider bulldozing the building?"

"I'm sure he would, but Althea wants to fix it up and use it for a warehouse." Harriet shrugged. "Problem is, she doesn't have much money and the bank wants a good-sized down payment before they'll finance the project. She's trying to use everything she can and cut corners wherever it's possible."

His mother used to do that with his clothes. Even now, Jared's toes cramped up when he recalled the pair of black loafers he'd had to wear to church every Sunday for four long years after they'd moved in with his uncle, until he'd no longer been able to force his feet into them. "If I do this, I'll do it right," he told Harriet. "Let's go see this place."

Located on a winding two-lane road ten minutes from Blairsville, the property Althea had picked out for the co-op reminded Jared of a ghost town, complete with a rutted parking lot overrun with weeds and debris. The building she intended to salvage listed to one side, as though waiting for the next strong wind to bring it down and send its rotting pieces tumbling down the mountain.

"I suppose you could shore it up, replace the roof," Harriet said, her tone interminably cheerful as she picked her way carefully with her high-heeled pumps over broken concrete where Jared imagined there once had been a pair of old-fashioned gas pumps.

He walked around the derelict building and pictured

it gone, replaced by a new, sturdy structure big enough for the craftspeople to do their work as well as store their products.

"Can trucks get in here?" he asked. He tried to recall whether any of the bridges they'd crossed had low weight limits. There was that tunnel down the road, too. He doubted that a tractor-trailer rig could make it through the low clearance.

"Big ones can't. That's one reason the property's so cheap. Althea said she'd buy a pickup truck, pack up orders here, then drive them to Blairsville for shipping."

His mother would have said Althea was planning to "make do," Jared thought as he thanked Harriet for showing him the place. Before they left, he made arrangements for her to show him some larger, more accessible properties the next day.

For the first twenty-some-odd years of his life, Jared had "made do," and when he'd earned his first million, he'd sworn he'd never settle again for less than what he wanted. If he were going to help Althea realize her dream, he'd see to it that her co-op would be first class from the start.

The hours crept by. Althea wondered if the day would ever end. She imagined Jared's quilt stretched over the big frame and pictured her needle darting in and out in the simple pattern she'd chosen for the borders, around the small rectangles that made up each colorful block. In her fantasy, she saw him take the needle from her hand, catch it in the fabric, lift her in his strong arms, and take her upstairs to his bed.

Her cheeks grew warm. A flame kindled inside her body. Tonight, nothing would stop them. She'd open to Jared, feel him fill her with himself. She would know the joy and the pain of being a woman grown. No more waiting and wondering. No more putting off pleasure for a day that might never come.

"Althea?"

She turned and saw Bea Elder. Hopefully the woman hadn't developed the ability to read minds. "I'm sorry. I was—woolgathering."

"No mind, girl. I just came to collect whatever you got for them two quilts. Wish you'd get that co-op off the ground. Don't know how I'm going to manage this winter. Leah and Sherry won't stop growing for long enough to wear out their sneakers, and that's the truth." Bea shrugged her skinny shoulders.

"Children do grow, don't they?"

"Those two sure do. Leah's not even twelve, and she's already taller than her ma." Bea's expression darkened, as though thinking about her runaway daughter cast a shadow across her weathered face.

"Speaking of Rachel, have you heard from her?" Althea hated to ask, yet thought it would be impolite not to. After all, she and Bea's daughter had gone to the country school together before Rachel ran off with a drummer from Augusta, the summer they were fourteen.

"She called a while back, said she'd come see the girls when she could. Lordy, I don't know why God couldn't have given me a good girl like you."

"I'm sorry she's hurt you, Ms. Bea." Althea fidgeted, uncomfortable with the idea that folks thought she was a plaster saint.

"Not your fault, Althea. Hear you've been seein' that city slicker who bought Big Bear Mountain lock, stock, and barrel."

Word traveled fast if it had gotten as far as the isolated group of cabins on Raccoon Ridge, where Bea lived. "We've gone out a few times." She hoped God wouldn't strike her down for not telling the whole truth.

"Watch yourself, girl. Don't you go gettin' taken in by his fast-talkin', the way my Rachel did. Can't trust city men, no way."

Althea figured she could trust Jared just fine to give her what she wanted and not expect the forever promises the local single men would demand. But she wanted to ease Bea's mind. "Jared's no city slicker. He was born on the mountain. He lived there until he was twelve years old, before his ma took him to his uncle's in Atlanta. His memories haunted him. Made him want to come back home."

Bea's mouth tightened, and her tired eyes took on a doubting expression. "All right. You just take care. I'd best be gettin' whatever you managed to sell those quilts for. I promised the girls some meat for supper tonight."

Reaching into the cash register, Althea counted out three hundred sixty dollars, then took two more twenties. Although she hadn't found a way yet to fund the co-op, she could afford to give up her usual ten percent commission for selling Bea's quilts. No question about it, Bea needed the forty dollars more than she did.

"This ought to help you out a bit," she said, as she handed Bea the money.

"Thanks. I'll spend a little of it with you. I need some batting and material for the backing of a full-size quilt I've got pieced at home. Do you think it'll sell faster than these two did?"

"Nothing ready-made's selling very well this summer," Althea said, hoping God wouldn't strike her down for the outright lie. She wasn't willing to hurt Bea by telling her it was nigh onto impossible to find buyers for her work. Mountain women did their own quilting, and most tourists with money to burn demanded the quality of design that Bea just wasn't capable of doing.

"Oh." The grizzled woman fingered a bolt of hot pink cotton cloth. "The one I've got to quilt's a crazy quilt. I used up a bunch of my scraps to piece it. Wouldn't this be nice for the backing?"

"If you're going to sell it, you'd be better off backing a crazy quilt with a neutral color. Maybe plain unbleached muslin." Althea could imagine the color dissonance Bea had probably created by piecing scraps of random materials and random shapes into a quilt top. Best to tone it down, not give it a backing that wouldn't go with ninety percent of people's bedrooms. "It's cheaper, too."

Bea's rheumy gaze focused on the hot pink material. "I like this. Lord knows, I'll be looking at it long enough while I'm doin' the quilting. I'll take enough to back a double-bed quilt. Batting, too. The Lord willing, I'll have this sewed up and back to you in a few weeks."

Althea watched Bea scurry out to her battered station wagon. Hoping the ancient vehicle hadn't breathed its last in front of her store, she listened to it choke and wheeze. When it came to life with a roar, she let out a sigh. A cloud of smoke hovered in the parking lot as Bea turned onto the highway.

Would Bea and other women like her be able to hold on until Althea found a way to finance the co-op? Or would they give up and move to the city to take the kind of dead-end job Jared's mother had endured?

She wondered if she'd ever be able to regain community support for the co-op. If she didn't, she might never be able to fulfill the dream she'd shared with Bill—to help women on their own to succeed while doing what they knew best, stay in their mountain homes, and still make a decent living.

The few thousand dollars she'd managed to save wouldn't go far—not even far enough to let her buy that deserted gas station Harriet Tucker had been trying to unload for years. Although the site was far from ideal, it would give the co-op a place to start.

Althea's thoughts slid back to Jared. He'd seemed interested when they talked about the co-op. She could ask for his advice . . .

No. She'd relied on Bill. When she'd lost him, she'd vowed never again to count on anybody but herself. She couldn't let herself think of Jared as anything but a passing fancy—an attractive man who would touch her life for a little while, breathe life back into it. And disappear.

She smiled as she turned off the lights and checked the doors to be certain they were locked. At her cabin while she changed clothes a few minutes later, Althea focused on Jared and the hot, sensual way he made her feel.

His magnificent body, all strength and sinew and impressive maleness. His heated green-gold gaze and sexy smile. No doubt about it, Jared was all man; yet she'd sensed remnants of the boy who'd grown up on Big Bear Mountain.

Althea was catering to that boy when she took a peach cobbler and a quart of vanilla ice cream out of her freezer and added them to the basket of sandwiches she'd made. Raindrops spattered her as she took their meal to her car.

TEN

Jared stepped onto the porch and listened to rain slam onto the cedar shingles as he watched for Althea's car. Anticipation sluiced through his veins, warming him despite the dampness and the cold.

The gentle stream had become a raging torrent of water pounding at the rocks on its banks as it raced down the mountain toward the river. A summer storm, here now and gone within the blink of an eye.

He remembered weather like this from his childhood. Soon raindrops would glitter in the sunshine that would peek out from behind deep gray clouds. Leaves of maples and hardwood trees would sparkle. The mist in the valley below would gleam with golden moisture in the twilight.

From his spot under the porch roof, he took a deep breath. The fresh smell of the forest and the rain heightened his senses. His pulse quickened when he spotted Althea's Pathfinder winding its way up Big Bear Mountain.

When she pulled up next to the porch, he bounded down the stairs and opened her car door. If it hadn't been for the split-oak picnic basket she thrust into his arms, he'd have kissed her where they stood, heedless of the rain pounding down on their heads.

Instead, he hurried her inside and to his bedroom, stripped off her wet clothes. When she was dry, he wrapped her in his thick terry cloth robe. "Warm enough?"

She smiled at him when he began taking off his own wet slacks and shirt. "I am now. I need to put some of our dinner in the oven."

"Go ahead. I'll change and meet you downstairs." He could wait. When they finally made love, he wanted to go slowly, savor each moment and each sensation. He didn't like the idea of rushing because something might be burning on the stove. He changed into dry jeans and a sweatshirt, then took the stairs two at the time.

Despite its being summer, dampness had cooled the dusky twilight air. Jared knelt, laid kindling and logs in the fireplace grate. He lit the kindling, blew on the flame until it began to spread.

"I love a fire," Althea said.

Jared turned, lifted his gaze, and smiled. Swathed neck to toe in his shapeless terry robe, Althea shouldn't have looked sexy, but she did. Earthy. Wanting. So beautiful she took his breath away. In slow motion, he prodded the fire, then set the poker on the hearth. When he stood, he held out both hands. "Sit with me."

He noticed after they sank onto the sofa that she'd fastened the quilt top into the frame he'd set up earlier. Centered between the fireplace and a floor-to-ceiling window, it lent a warm, personal touch to the room.

Some fruity, spicy smell wafted from the kitchen. It tickled his taste buds and made his mouth water. His house felt like home tonight. Althea's warm body, tucked close to his, soothed as much as aroused him.

"What's cooking?" he asked.

"Peach cobbler."

"Smells great."

She snuggled closer, nuzzled his neck, slid her fingers under the neckband of his sweatshirt. "It'll be a half hour before supper's ready."

"Not long enough for what I've got in mind." Jared wanted to take his time. He needed to drive Althea as crazy as she made him. "Let's relax and listen to the rain."

She nipped at his earlobe, then pulled away and looked him in the eye. "The rain is almost like a song, you know. Sometimes wild, other times as soft as a whisper." She paused and leaned against the back of the sofa.

He noticed her eyelids flutter, then close. "It's a lover's rain tonight. Our rain," she said, her voice dreamy.

The storm was letting up. Pounding raindrops gave way to gentle taps against the roof. Soft droplets tinkled against the windowpanes. The rising moon shone silver against the crystal raindrops and made them glisten like ice in the firelight.

"You're right," he murmured as he rubbed the unbelievably silky skin on the inside of her wrist.

How could he ever have thought Althea anything but beautiful? Jared met her pale blue gaze. When he did, he sensed her desire. Desire for him.

There was something about her. Something that

made him believe that with her he could be twice the man he'd ever been. He'd be damned if he knew what it was, but he sensed she could bring out whatever it was that he'd locked up inside him—that elusive quality no woman, not even Marcie, had ever managed to unleash.

Suddenly he knew. For the first time in his life, his hormones had gotten tied up with emotions. That was what had him panting after Althea like a teenage boy about to have his first sexual encounter.

He found himself wanting to do more than satisfy her in bed. More than enjoy mindless sex. He wanted to give her everything she wanted, take care of her. Make her forget the boy she'd loved who died and left her all alone.

He wanted to give her a sensual banquet, a feast that would make every one she'd had before pale in her memory and leave her savoring only him. The sight of them locked together as close as a man and woman could ever get. The sound of him saying her name when he erupted deep inside her. Their mingled tastes and smells, and the feel of his body around her, in her. When he felt himself begin to harden against his zipper, he fought to maintain control.

A half hour later, Althea watched Jared lift the last bite of dessert from his plate. He brought the peach cobbler, dripping with remnants of melted ice cream, from his bowl to his lips. Slowly, he closed his mouth around the sweet, tangy treat. Then he swallowed. With his tongue, he captured one last drop off the corner of his mouth.

The grin he shot her as he got up from the table was positively predatory. Her breath caught in her throat. Suddenly she wasn't as certain as before that this was where she wanted to be. "Would you like me to make coffee?" she asked.

"No."

She'd noticed a six-pack of beer in his refrigerator. "Want a beer?"

"No."

"More dessert?"

"Althea, what I want now is you. All night, with no interruptions. Just the rain, the firelight, and the two of us." Slowly, deliberately, he pulled back her chair, then lifted her into his arms.

"The dishes. I should at least put them in—"

"Forget the dishes." He kissed her. His tongue slipped between her teeth and entwined with hers. Vaguely she realized they were leaving the kitchen, heading back toward the sofa in front of the cozy fire.

He set her down, then joined her. He covered her with his body, pressed her into the soft leather cushions. His kiss went on and on. It stole her breath and made her push aside the doubts that had flooded her mind as they finished their dessert.

He tasted like peaches, cinnamon, and vanilla. And something else. A flavor uniquely his. As he slipped his hand inside her robe and cupped her breast, she realized she'd never again eat peach cobbler without associating it with Jared.

Sparks flew inside her when he pinched her nipple lightly, then rolled it between his thumb and forefinger.

Like the rest of him, his fingers had a rough-smooth edge—hard and strong, yet gentle when he touched her.

His heart pounded against her breasts. His breath came faster when he finally broke their kiss. His eyes glowed green-gold in the firelight, and his tanned cheeks glistened. When he met her gaze, she felt a sense of urgency in him that was at odds with his leisurely exploration of her body. A need that matched her own.

Did she look that way, too? She felt a breeze and guessed she, too, had a sheen of moisture on her brow. Then he untied her robe and pulled the edges apart. When he dipped his head to her breast and took an aching nipple in his mouth, she couldn't think at all.

She felt tight. Empty. Moisture built up between her legs, and she tingled as though every nerve end in her body were on fire. He nibbled gently at one breast, then gave the other equal time as he stroked her from neck to waist. He made her squirm with need for more. For him.

Not Bill. The arousing touches they had shared were only bittersweet memories. Jared was real. Alive. He was here now, awakening sensations she'd never fully explored. Ones she would discover soon, for Jared had no hang-ups about waiting for some nebulous day in the future, a future which had never come for her and Bill.

They would merge her softness with Jared's strength, soon. Tonight. Not someday. She felt his hardness against her belly, and she wanted him now.

She wanted to see him, to explore his big, hard body.

She wanted to touch the rigid column of his sex. Impatient, she twisted around and reached for his zipper.

With one hand, he stilled her. "Not yet. I want you ready."

"I am."

Smiling, Jared kissed the tip of her nose. "You aren't now, but you soon will be. Trust me."

She did. Implicitly. He'd give her pleasure, not pain. Leaning back, she gave him free rein of her body. She savored the heat from the fire and the feelings his touches evoked as he learned her with his hands and mouth.

She shivered. Every nerve in her body tingled. She wanted more. When he slipped a hand between her legs, she parted them, anxious for his intimate touch. Her eyelids closed.

The sounds of the fire and the rain blurred together, then faded. No sight, no sound, no taste. Just the musky smell of lovers, and the feel of Jared's talented fingers coaxing new, explosive sensation from the tiny nub of nerves no one, not even she, had ever before explored.

Arching her hips to him, she sought something just beyond her reach. The pressure built inside her, so fierce she had to find release. He shifted, put his mouth where his fingers had been, flicked her with his tongue, then closed his lips and suckled her there, the way he'd sampled her breasts. The sensations mounted, almost unbearable in their intensity.

"Stop. Please. Don't . . . don't stop." Althea's world exploded in a kaleidoscope of rainbow hues as she gasped for breath. Jared lifted his head, met her gaze. He smiled. Then he bent to her again, resumed giving her the most intimate of kisses. When she reached another climax, he lifted her, carried her upstairs, and laid her on his bed.

The rain beat gently on the roof of the loft, breaking the silence. While he undressed, Jared never took his eyes off Althea. As soon as he was naked, he shut off all but one dim lamp, slipped on a condom, and stretched out beside her on the bed.

Suddenly he was unsure of himself. What made him think he could measure up against a man Althea had obviously loved, a man made invincible in death?

"Are you sure?" He wasn't going to last long. He was hard as rock, desperate to make her his own.

"Make love to me, Jared."

Her crystal blue gaze met his, full of passion and promise. He couldn't wait any longer. Trembling with the effort to hold back, he positioned himself and thrust into her tight, wet sheath. Something blocked his path, then suddenly gave way. Her gasp made him cringe. The truth tore at his heart.

She was a virgin.

Regret warring with awe, he kissed away her tears. "Sweetheart, I'm sorry." He gritted his teeth, forced himself to be still, to give her time to recover.

"It's all right. I wanted you to . . ."

"Be your first? You should have told me. I could have . . ." He'd hurt her. Made her cry. Jared wished he could take her pain and make it his own. "I'd have been more careful. Made it better for you."

"Hush. It's all right. More than all right." She shifted and took him deeper into her body.

He gritted his teeth, prayed for control. Mindful of her tenderness, he tempered his thrusts. While his body screamed for him to slam into her again and again, to hurry and find release, he rocked his hips against her slowly, gently.

She felt so hot. So tight. When she opened to him and wrapped her legs around his hips, he gritted his teeth. She began to move to his rhythm, at first tentatively, then with more assurance. The sweet, hot friction built until he could hardly bear it.

He held on as long as he could. Primal urges took over, though, made him seek to fill. To conquer. His whole body shaking, he gave up, exploded in her at the moment he felt her inner muscles constrict as she reached her own zenith.

Exhausted, he rolled to his side, taking her with him and holding her close. The tears he felt on her cheeks reminded him of the gentle rain.

Incredible. He'd have never thought being the first would matter, but it did. Althea's gift awed Jared, convinced him she must love him. He could do worse than take her, make her his own forever, not just for this night.

He lay beside her, thinking. Intermittently throughout the night, he dozed. As he looked through a window at the gently falling rain, he listened to the soft cadence of her breathing and planned how he'd win her. He'd bind her to him with ties of gentle emotions, not the business connections he'd once thought would cement him to Marcie.

He was fairly certain Althea would hate Atlanta. No matter. They'd spend most of their time here. He'd keep his condo for those times he couldn't take care of details over the phone or on the computer. On those trips, he'd see that she had fun, take her to shows—

He came up short. Did she like musicals? Drama? Comedy? He had no idea what Althea cared about, except for quilting and the co-op she'd planned to run with the boy she'd loved but never slept with.

She was hardly more than a stranger. A stranger who was making him a quilt and showing him around the mountains he'd stayed away from for twenty-some-odd years. A stranger who'd given him a precious gift he didn't deserve.

It was a bit premature to be thinking of engagement rings and eternal vows. But Jared would get that co-op going for her. All it would take was money, and he had plenty. Maybe his accountant could come up with a way he could deduct whatever he'd spend on it.

Stirring in her sleep, Althea pulled one hand out from under the covers. Jared reached over and clasped her hand. What kind of ring would she like? he wondered. Then he caught himself. Not now. Not yet. Maybe not ever.

What they might both be feeling was a healthy dose of lust. After all, she'd made it clear from the day they spent together in Helen that she wasn't looking for anything permanent.

"Jared?" Eyes still closed, she rolled over against his side.

His sex hardened and swelled, as though they hadn't made love just a few hours earlier. "Morning, sweetheart," he said, as he aligned their bodies, stroked her back. "Are you all right?"

"Perfect." She snuggled closer, rubbed her lips along the side of his neck. "Is making love always as good as it was last night?"

"God, I hope so." He hesitated to ask, yet had to know. "Althea, why me?"

"Why me what? Oh, you mean—"

"Why'd you pick me to be your first lover?"

She traced the seam of his lips with a forefinger. Her smile revealed nothing except, he hoped, satisfaction.

"You turn me on. You've got to know, you're one sexy guy."

He felt sexy as hell this morning, and he wanted nothing more than to roll over her, make love all over again. Still, he had to ask one question. "Why didn't you sleep with—"

"Bill? We'd decided to wait until we were married. Well, that day never came, and I promised myself after he died that if I ever found myself wanting to make love with someone, I'd do it then and there. Life's too short."

Her eyes welled with tears, but she shifted her lower body and cradled his erection between her thighs.

She must have loved this Bill. She'd planned to share her life with him. Logical deduction told Jared she must love him now. He didn't know whether to shout with joy or tremble with fear. Speechless, he let his action speak for itself. He bent his head and took her nipple in his mouth.

"Please." When she reached down and gave him an intimate caress, she smiled. "Come inside me," she whispered close to his ear, then flicked his earlobe with her tongue.

He flexed his hips, seated himself in her. At the same time, he kissed her, thrusting his tongue in her mouth with the rhythm they set. The side-by-side position didn't allow deep penetration. It and the slow pace they set teased him, made him want more. It felt good to savor the sensations of being joined so intimately. He wished he could prolong the delicious torture forever.

For a long time, he loved her that way. When he'd taken all he could stand, he rolled her to her back. His control lost, he plunged hard and deep. Soon her climax triggered his own.

"I'm going to have to get some quilting done tonight," Althea said with a big grin before she left for the shop.

Jared started to suggest she hire the woman with the grandkids to finish his quilt so she could spend her own spare time satisfying him in bed. Then he thought he'd better hold his tongue. "All right. I'll check out a new game or two while you work. And I'll fix dinner tonight." If he had his way, that quilt might not get finished before winter—some winter several years in the future.

After Althea left, Jared got up and called Harriet Tucker. He checked in with his company's accounting manager while he waited for the realtor to arrive with a list of possible co-op sites that met the requirements he'd laid out.

He could hardly wait to surprise Althea with the ideal place to realize her dream.

Althea wouldn't have believed the way Jared made her feel if someone had tried to explain it to her before last night. She hoped she wasn't blushing now, but her cheeks felt awfully warm. Smiling at the middle-aged tourist who'd come into the shop looking for a Wedding Ring quilt, she tried to put the delicious feelings she'd just discovered out of her mind.

"Did you make this quilt?"

Althea focused her gaze on the woman's well-kept face, then glanced at the big diamond ring that weighed down her left hand. "What? Oh, yes." She'd spent most of her evenings last winter piecing and quilting the king-size quilt that seemed to attract more than its share of admirers, but so far hadn't sold.

"How much is it?"

The price tag was there, in plain sight. "A thousand dollars." That would go a long way toward fattening Althea's down payment on the land for the co-op, she thought as she tried to guess whether the woman would pay her price.

"I meant, what will you take for it?" Her customer slid a perfectly manicured hand across a point of the star. The stone in her ring caught the sunlight that filtered through the window. Shards of reflected light made the jewel-toned fabrics glow.

"A thousand dollars." This woman didn't look as though she needed a discount.

She frowned, then shrugged. "All right. It will be perfect in my guest room."

No one else came in the store before lunchtime, leaving Althea free to savor the memories of the past night—and Jared. She loved the way he'd kissed and suckled her in the most delicious secret places . . . and how he'd made her beg for more. Last night Jared had coaxed out sensations she'd never felt before, not even with Bill.

She figured it had to be a myth that sex was better

when one was in love, but she spared a moment to regret that she and Bill had missed their chance to experience the joy she'd shared with Jared.

Her memories had dulled with time, but she recalled the mildly pleasant feelings Bill's tentative touches had evoked. Would he have been able to take her to the heights Jared had?

ELEVEN

Jared had never felt better. He breathed in cool mountain air still damp from the rain as he followed Harriet's Cadillac sedan in his sports coupe. The wind blew his hair, and that reminded him how good Althea's fingers felt when she'd tangled them in the strands of hair above his ears and held him to her while he tasted her honey.

The last place Harriet took him to had promise—plenty of acreage and access for shippers. It even boasted a sturdy warehouse that had been built a few years back, then abandoned when its owners went belly-up. Jared didn't like it much, though, because it lay several miles northeast of Blairsville. If they put the co-op there, Althea would have a long, treacherous drive from Big Bear Mountain.

Mentally Jared crossed his fingers. The site where they were heading now was less than three miles from his place, about as close to Dahlonega as it was to Blairsville. When Harriet pulled in at the junction of the highway and a secondary road, he followed, then stopped his car.

"You could put a good-sized building here," Harriet said, gesturing toward a concrete slab that bore traces of some construction that was long gone. "Slab's no good, I'm afraid."

The cracked concrete didn't look as if it would hold up under Jared's weight, much less support a building. "You said this site has ten acres?"

"Yes. The plot's nearly square. It could handle several buildings the size Althea has in mind. Zoning's for light industry because of that quarry across the road. The owner will probably deal—the land has been on the market nearly two years."

"He'll have to. His asking price is way too high. Make a verbal offer. Start out at five thousand an acre," Jared said, aware the owner was asking nearly three times that. "If I have to, I'll go as high as ten thousand an acre, but I'd like to get it for seven."

No way was this land worth ten thousand an acre. For a manufacturing business, it was fine; but it wasn't worth a damn for vacation housing or as a tourist attraction, not with the rock quarry across the road that made for a less than scenic vista.

"You want me to make an offer on this?" Harriet looked perplexed. "There's no way Althea can get a loan big enough to finance this property, let alone build on it."

"There won't be a loan. And the offer's coming from Cain Software, not from Althea."

The woman gaped. "You're going to . . ." Then she smiled. "Althea must be thrilled."

"Not me. My company. We'll buy this land, build whatever kind of facility is needed. We'll give it to the co-op and take a tax write-off. I understand things like that are done all the time." Jared smiled, glad his accountant had explained this morning how making Althea's dream come true could actually save Cain Software thousands in federal and state income taxes.

Harriet shook her head. "Maybe in Atlanta, but not around here."

Suddenly Jared remembered what else Harriet just said. "By the way, Althea doesn't know I'm doing this just yet. I want to surprise her."

Harriet looked him in the eye, her expression conveying alarm. "You'd better run this by her. That girl has a bundle of pride. I doubt she'll sit still while you hand her what she's been rock-hard-headed determined to put together all by herself."

The realtor's words gave Jared a moment of discomfort. Then he discounted them. Althea had never expected to build her co-op singlehandedly. He couldn't see what difference it would make whether the money to get the co-op established came from him or in bits and pieces from dozens of businesses in Blairsville and Dahlonega.

"Just make the offer," he said, giving the site one last look. "And let me know right away what the owner says."

Harriet shot him a dubious look, but she assured Jared she'd tender his offer. "I'll call you as soon as I can get with him," she told him as she climbed into her car. "If we can agree on a price, I'll draw up a contract—unless you'd rather leave that to your attorneys."

"I'd better. The accountant says the papers have to be done a certain way if we're going to get a tax write-off." With that, Jared slid into his car and started the engine.

The secondary road wound around a mountain, past

a sparkling lake. When he saw an angler snag a good-size trout, Jared's mouth watered. He'd fix a trout dinner tonight, complete with fat French fries, hush puppies, and cole slaw like his mother used to make.

"Damn." Jared hadn't the first notion of how to fry a fish, let alone make a hush puppy or the creamy dressing that used to make his mom's cole slaw taste special. As he negotiated a hairpin curve, he considered taking Althea out for dinner, but discarded that notion.

Their relationship was too new and too compelling for him to want to share her, even for the time it would take them to eat at a restaurant. He'd stick with his original plan, to bake the frozen lasagna he'd found on his last trip to the grocery store in Blairsville.

To take his mind off the mouth-watering trout dinner he didn't see in his immediate future, he visualized the co-op. The thought of a group of mountain women visiting as they worked on crafts they'd learned at their mothers' knees made him smile.

They'd need open, airy rooms, with plenty of natural light and space for projects in the making, he decided when he recalled the way his mom had squinted when she'd worked on a quilt or woven a basket next to the single window in their old cabin. He made a mental note to specify big windows, and maybe skylights, too.

By the time Jared pulled into his garage, he had a fair idea of what he thought Althea's co-op should look like. He'd also changed his mind about eating out. He'd take her to that rustic place on the highway that led to Blairsville, the one where the smell of frying trout had seduced his taste buds when he drove by it. The lasagna could stay in his freezer to feed them another day.

Six o'clock came faster than Althea would have expected. Trina's sister-in-law, Ellen Wells, had come in after lunch. It had been all Althea could do not to cry when Ellen laid three show quilts on the counter, then related her sad story.

Apparently Ellen's husband had cleaned out their meager savings two weeks ago, before he took off for parts unknown. Now Ellen had four hungry kids and nothing to feed them with, except the fancy quilts she'd hoped to win money prizes with at craft fairs in the fall.

Nothing could have kept Althea from using the money she'd made before lunchtime to buy two of those quilts. When she'd sell them, she had no idea. Single bed quilts were slow movers, especially when they weren't matched pairs and weren't patterns suitable for children's rooms. But that hadn't been a consideration when she'd heard Ellen tell about her plight.

Althea shook her head as she climbed into her car. The reality of a co-op seemed always to stay a stone's throw out of reach. Still, she couldn't sleep nights if she didn't help out where she could, keep some child from going to bed hungry or another from going barefoot when she outgrew her shoes. Maybe she should ask Jared to help, not try to do it all on her own.

She couldn't. Letting him share her dream would bring them too close. Too personal. If she weren't careful she could care too much, so much that losing him would tear her apart. It wasn't just death that could grab Jared; it was life. His life in Atlanta. Hers here.

He could get bored with the slow pace of life on Big Bear Mountain at any time. He could leave her as surely as Bill had gone to heaven. She couldn't risk hurting like that again, but she had a funny feeling she'd stepped across the line. She'd given too much of herself already to the man who showed her the kinds of pleasure she'd only dreamed about until last night.

Too bad her church was so poor. She glanced at the small building as she drove by. Grateful for the small pledge of support the pastor had made, she wished she could get similar pledges from a few businessmen in Dahlonega and Blairsville. If she did, the bank might be willing to lend its support. Everyone seemed to think the co-op was a good idea, but not many people were willing to put their money on the line until she'd proven it could support itself.

A vicious circle, one without end. When she got out of her car in Jared's driveway, Althea shoved her dream of helping women help themselves to the back of her mind. Pushing her worries aside would have been much more difficult if not for the tingling anticipation she felt at the thought of spending another night in his intimate embrace.

"Come on, we're going to get fried rainbow trout at this place I spotted on the highway south of Blairsville." Jared sounded as excited as a little boy.

Althea had to suppress a laugh. This was a facet of

the man that she hadn't experienced before. "You don't mean Uncle Ed's, do you?"

"I think that's the name of the place. It's a long, narrow building on the west side of the road, not too far from town. I'm starving." He helped her out of her Pathfinder, practically dragged her to his car.

She chuckled when he gunned the engine and pretended to speed down the mountain road. "I take it Uncle Ed's found another customer. He does make the best fried rainbow trout around here. They catch a lot of them in the Nottely River, right behind the restaurant."

"Do they serve hush puppies?"

"Hot and greasy, with lots of onion."

"Just the way I like them." Jared turned onto the highway and set a steady pace. "What's that place over there?"

Althea turned in the direction he indicated and looked at four perfectly round ponds nestled close together in a valley. "They're trout ponds. Lots of folks farm trout. They harvest them and sell them to packing houses and restaurants."

"Good business, if everybody goes nuts for trout the way I do." He pulled into the parking lot at Uncle Ed's Place, then hurried around the car to open her door. "I'm looking forward to this," he told her as they waited at the door for a table overlooking the river.

When she glanced around, she saw several people she knew. It felt strange, being here with Jared for everybody to see. She and Bill had eaten here a couple of times every month, then lingered over sweet iced tea to visit with their friends.

"There's somebody over there waving at you." Jared whispered close to her ear, then gestured toward a table in the corner.

"That's Trina Wells, the woman who pieced your quilt." She was also one of the most efficient bearers of gossip in a fifty-mile radius. Any hope that her presence here would be ignored died when Althea met Trina's attentive gaze. "Her husband's name is Joe."

"I don't remember them. But then I don't recall a lot of people I must have known when I was a kid." Jared put a hand at Althea's waist, and they followed the waitress to their table.

Althea thought she sensed regret in Jared's simple statement. After they'd ordered their dinner, she pointed out other people she knew. Jared recalled only a few, and he appeared to recognize none except by name.

"Do you come here often?" he asked.

Their meals had just arrived, and already five people had stopped by their table. Althea guessed Jared had good reason to assume she hung out here all the time. "I used to," she said, her gaze on his sensual lips as he sipped from a big plastic glass of sweetened iced tea.

"With the man you were going to marry?"

"Yes. He loved Uncle Ed's fried trout." Althea waited for the familiar grief to overwhelm her. When it didn't, she shared the memory with Jared.

"We used to come here all the time. I used to tease Bill and complain that this was the only place he knew to take me." The feeling that washed over her was sad and sweet, no longer painful.

"So, now everybody's coming around, checking out

your new man, I guess." Jared took a big bite of fish, then popped a hush puppy into his mouth.

"I guess so."

"How do you think I measure up?"

Althea smiled. She tried to push aside the thought that half the people she'd grown up with would soon be deluging her with warnings about city slickers, while the other half would be offering advice as to how best to catch the big fish they'd seen nibbling at her hook. "You measure up just fine. You don't have a thing to worry about."

"Good. Eat your dinner before it gets cold." With that, Jared followed his own advice, dug into his trout and trimmings until his plate was empty.

Althea managed to eat about half of her food. She never had been able to enjoy eating while folks stared at her. By the time they got back to find three teenagers drooling over Jared's Mercedes in the parking lot, at least fifteen more people she knew had come over to remind her of old times here. Times she'd tried to banish from her memory.

"Let's go home."

Althea had never heard three words she agreed with more.

TWELVE

The after-dinner drive to Big Bear Mountain with Althea at his side and the walk they took afterward along a path that paralleled the stream lent a feeling of permanence—a sense of rightness to the summer evening.

Twilight hadn't yet darkened the shaded path. Jared knelt, picked up a chunk of rocky pyrite the heavy runoff had left at the edge of the path. "Fool's gold," he said, handing the nugget to Althea.

"Looks real enough."

He wondered if the feelings he had for her were the real thing, not an illusion. He hoped yet feared that he was chasing his future, not following a dream as elusive as the one that had claimed his dad so long ago.

"Can't always tell something by the way it looks," he said.

Althea smiled. "I guess not."

She'd been quiet tonight. Too quiet. "You've got something weighing on your mind. Want to tell me what it is?"

"Just a friend and her problems. Her husband left her and their kids with not a penny to their names. I bought a couple of quilts from her this afternoon."

"Anything we can do to help her out?" He remembered how he'd felt when he was twelve, knowing his father had left him and his mom alone and broke. The fact that Dad had died, not run off, hadn't made any difference in the way losing its breadwinner had affected his family.

She looked up at him, her expression troubled. "I don't know what, beyond buying her quilts. I already did that. She wouldn't take outright charity. All she has to hold onto is her pride."

Tears glittered in her pale eyes, and he couldn't help but see how her friend's plight distressed her.

"We'd better go back inside," she said. "I need to get some quilting done tonight."

Pride. Until he'd come home, he had practically forgotten about mountain folks and their stiff-necked pride. Harriet's warning rang in his head, made him rethink the wisdom of telling Althea now that he planned to make her dream of a craft co-op come true. He'd wait, not take a chance that the realtor might be right about how Althea would react—at least until he could put a deed to the land into her hands.

Birds chirped in the trees overhead. In the distance Jared heard some creature's plaintive call. "You really want to work on the quilt?" he asked as they climbed the steep incline that led to his front porch. "I can think of more pleasant ways to spend a lazy summer night."

Althea met his gaze, then gave his hand a squeeze. "I promised to finish it by September. I keep my promises."

Her soft lips tempted him too much. No way could he resist taking her in his arms. He held her under the twilight sky, beneath the towering branches of trees that had grown on the mountainside centuries before they were born. Trees that would still be there long after they were dead and gone.

For a long time they stood there, their bodies aligned. Lips fused, tongues exploring. Lovers in their cocoon, insignificant in the total scheme of nature but an entire world to each other.

Did she share his wonder, sense the connection between them? He hoped so. When Althea pulled back, Jared felt as though he'd lost part of himself.

Jared made Althea want things she'd promised herself she'd never risk again. Love. Commitment. Promises for a lifetime. Promises fate had a way of breaking.

While he'd held her earlier, she'd let herself go for a little while. She'd savored the safety and the protection of his strong arms, and the heat of his hard man's body. Now, as she made tiny stitches in the quilt he would use to ward off winter's cold, she watched him look up from his laptop computer, then stare out the window into the night.

He turned to her and smiled, then set the computer on the table. With agile grace that reminded her of a stalking panther, he got up and crossed the room. Like a supplicant, he knelt at her feet on the deep green, gold, and ivory braided rug that reminded her of the color of his eyes.

"Go on with your quilting, sweetheart. I'm just going to make you feel good." His husky words washed over her like honey.

He took off her sandals and massaged first one foot

and ankle, then the other. Slowly, then faster and harder, his fingers moved in a rhythm she would always associate with making love. With Jared.

His lips followed the path where his hands had worked their magic. Up her calves and past the hem of her long, loose skirt. The rasp of his callused fingers on the backside of her knees set off a jolt of need. Her insides turned to liquid fire. To keep her sanity, she tried to concentrate on stitching around a patchwork block.

"Slide this way a little, sweetheart." He sounded hoarse—congested. The way she felt inside. His big hands at her hipbones scalded her with their heat as he coaxed her to the edge of the chair.

"Raise up," he said.

When she did, he slid her plain cotton panties down and off. He raked his thumbs across her belly, through the soft hair on her trembling mound and lower. With agile fingers he teased the sensitive flesh on her upper thighs until she opened to him.

She watched him position her skirt high on her thighs and gaze at the secret place between her legs that not even she had ever seen so closely. Embarrassed yet unbelievably aroused, she spread her legs wider to give him better access.

"You're beautiful here, too. Wet and warm and irresistible. And mine. I've got to taste you." His head disappeared under her skirt as he opened her wide with his thumbs and flicked her tingling little knot of nerves with his tongue. Then he took her in his mouth.

She couldn't summon the will to dispute his possessive claim. What he was doing felt too good. Pressure mounted low in her belly, so fierce it made her drop her needle and grasp the chair arms to keep from floating away on a cloud of pure sensation. Suddenly she went numb, as though every nerve in her body had settled between her legs.

Feelings so intense they hurt, yet so delicious she wanted them to go on forever, radiated. They taunted her as he intensified the pressure, then paused to flick his tongue over her flesh and lap her honey.

Sweat beaded on her forehead. She gasped for breath. "Too much. No. Don't. Don't stop." What did she want? She didn't know. Then she came in a mighty jumble of sensations, overwhelming in their intensity.

"More?" he asked, the word muffled by her hiked-up skirt.

His warm breath tightened her still-throbbing flesh and kept her consciousness centered between her legs. How could he sound so calm? "I'll die."

"What a way to go, though." He tasted her again, then lifted his head. Still on his knees, he met her gaze. The look of stark need on his lean, hard face made her ache to satisfy it.

She cupped his cheeks between her palms, then rubbed her thumbs over his warm, moist skin. The raspy feel of his beard stubble against her palms was just one more thing she loved about this man.

Bending down, she repeated what he'd said to her. "Let me make you feel good, Jared."

Did he tense up at her whispered suggestion or did she only imagine she'd felt his facial muscles tighten beneath her fingers?

"Let's go to bed." He stood and scooped her up in his arms in one fluid motion.

THIRTEEN

God, but Jared craved her touch. More than anything, he wanted to let go, to feel Althea's hands and mouth on him, to let her touch him the way he'd just touched her. Her gaze scorched his flesh, made him impossibly hard, hotter than he'd ever been before. He watched her undress, then shrugged out of his shirt before shoving his jeans and boxers down.

Damn! He toed off dock shoes he'd forgotten he was wearing, then stepped out of the pants that had bunched at his ankles. Althea sat on the bed, her arms outstretched toward him. Two steps, maybe three, that was all it would take. He'd be in her arms. Under her spell.

But he couldn't lose control, not completely. He had the sinking feeling that he would if he gave in and put his pleasure in her soft, capable hands. He'd never let anyone have that much control over him. Could he open up that much, risk the self-control that had helped him forge a fortune from nothing? He'd worked too hard, and come so far, to give himself up so easily.

He took one step forward, then met her gaze. He'd never known there could be fire in ice, but there was. Her pale eyes glowed, burned as she raked him from head to toe with a gaze of crystal fire.

He couldn't resist her siren's call. He'd never cared so much before, never had so much to lose by holding himself aloof. Since he was twelve years old, he'd never missed anyone he lost, not even Marcie.

But he knew he'd miss Althea if she ever left him. He'd never cared for anyone the way he was coming to care for her. One more step, and he sank shamelessly onto the bed. Into her waiting arms.

She stroked his shoulders, his chest, his belly. Her every gentle touch stoked the fire inside him. His skin tingled in the wake of her touch. His heart pounded out a quickening cadence. His nose twitched, full of the smell of musk and woman and his own arousal.

Somewhere in the distance a timber wolf howled his mating call, a sound not too different from the groan he heard rumble from his own tight throat when she took his sex in her soft hands. She explored his length and thickness with gentle fingers. Her breath tickled his belly. In a futile effort to retain some semblance of self-control, he clenched his abdominal muscles.

When she touched him with her tongue, he nearly exploded. He steeled himself. For what seemed like hours but couldn't have been more than a few seconds, he endured the sweet torture of her hot, wet mouth. He could take no more. Before he lost himself completely, he took command.

Possession. The salt-tinged taste and satiny feel of Jared's male flesh still fresh on her tongue, Althea wrapped her legs around his hard-muscled hips. She welcomed him as he plunged into her so hard and deep it seemed as if they'd merged into one body. One heart.

Surrender. He demanded, she complied. He delved harder and deeper with each thrust. The fire that simmered low in her belly grew hotter. When he withdrew, she clenched her inner muscles as if she could hold him there.

He possessed her now. He held her with a sexual magnet she couldn't deny. He ravaged her mouth, stole her breath. Tiny explosions flared deep inside her. They intensified, strengthened, then centered where their bodies were joined in a powerful burst that overwhelmed her.

Caught up as she was in sensations beyond her wildest dreams, she barely heard his triumphant shout. For a long time Althea lay in the cradle of Jared's arms, sated and content.

The next day Althea waited on customers as though she were a zombie. Her energy depleted and her mind full of remembered sensations, she tried in vain to persuade herself that what she felt with Jared was only physical. She tried to focus only on his hard, lean body and the rasp of his beard stubble on her most sensitive flesh. The contrast between his rigid, pulsing sex and the velvety skin that gloved it. Satin over steel. The feel of him stroking deep inside her.

Then emotion would intrude. She'd see his face, taut with need, intense with something more than passion. Caring. Did he love her?

No. He couldn't, any more than she could love him. She wouldn't let him. They'd had the past two nights, and they would have as many more as fate allowed.

Great sex. Fun sex. Sex that blew her mind. But only sex, never anything more.

Tonight she had to go to Jim's place. She'd promised to take Gracie so he wouldn't have to watch the toddler on top of taking care of Mary and the baby for the first few days they were home from the hospital. Maybe, if she were lucky, she'd find that when it came to Jared, out of sight was out of mind.

"Althea?"

She looked up, embarrassed to have let Trina see her crinkling a patchwork block between nervous fingers. "What brings you here today?" she asked, forcing her fingers to be still, to stop torturing innocent fabrics.

"When I talked to you at Uncle Ed's last night, you said you needed me to work this afternoon."

Althea forced a smile. "Oh. That's right." Trina must think she was losing her mind.

The older woman dug into the quilted shopping bag she always carried. "Brought you a jar from the first batch of jelly this year." She held the small diamond-cut jelly glass up to the light and let out a sigh of apparent satisfaction at its dark purple, almost translucent color. "I'm about out of these pretty labels you made for me over at school. Could you get into the building and run off a few more for me?"

Althea nodded, then shook her head. "Not until August. The school board has the building locked up, now that they've finished the repairs." She should really get her own computer and not rely on using the only one at the last kindergarten-through-high school country school left in Georgia. If she did, though, she'd be another step farther away from having the down payment to get the co-op started.

Trina glanced at the neat white label. For a moment, she looked disappointed. Then she smiled. "No mind. I can always write them out myself, the way I did before."

Trina's handwritten labels looked sloppy. Althea was certain they hurt her sales, because she'd heard women comment, then pass on buying the jelly with the handwritten labels. She considered going to Dahlonega and having the print shop make a few labels—or she could ask Jared. He had a computer. Maybe he'd . . ." I'll get some labels for you."

Trina looked up from the cup of coffee she'd just poured. "You think you can get into the school? I'll go buy those blank labels you feed through the machine."

"Not at school. Jared has a computer at his house. I could ask him if I can use it."

A flurry of customers saved Althea from having to explain all the electronic marvels she'd seen in Jared's summer home on Big Bear Mountain. They didn't save her from thinking, though, how unfair it was that some folks had so much, others so little.

That thought stayed with her. It muted but didn't overwhelm the memories of sensual delights that thrummed through her body and filled her mind. After all, she told herself, Jared Cain had started out life with no more, and maybe less, than Trina. He'd earned his luxuries, and he deserved them as much as anyone else who'd worked hard to get ahead.

Could she ask Jared to make Trina's labels? Althea had no doubt he'd do it. He was that kind of man—generous and caring. Besides, it was a small-enough task, one that wouldn't take much time or effort.

She hated to ask, though. Asking for help would

erode her independence. It would start her on the track of relying on him to help her do what she had to accomplish on her own. Labels were a small thing; yet to Althea they were symbolic of all she was trying to do. By letting Jared into her dream, even in a small way like making labels for Trina's jelly glasses, she'd open the door to relying on him. If she weren't careful, she could find herself depending on him as much as she'd ever depended on Bill.

"Althea."

She blinked, then glanced across the counter at Trina. The other woman must be wondering about her sanity by now. "I'm sorry."

"I'd say that man's got you tied up in knots, girl."

"Don't be ridiculous." Trina had to make mountains out of molehills and smell romance where none existed. "I was just thinking about the co-op, and how I might get enough money to start it up this year."

"If that's what's bothering you, ask your boyfriend. I was pretty worried about you 'til I saw you together last night; but that man's a mighty good-looking devil, city slicker or not. And from the way he was looking at you, you've got him pretty darn near hooked."

"Hooked? I don't think so. We're friends."

"You spend four straight nights with your friends, girl? I thought better of you."

Althea felt her cheeks getting hot, but she held her ground. "Who on earth told you that?"

"You haven't been home at night since you two went racin' down to Atlanta together, the night Mary had the baby. Most of us weren't born yesterday." Hands on her hips, Trina stared Althea down.

Must everyone between Dahlonega and Blairsville

poke their noses into her personal, private business? Althea fought back annoyance, reminded herself this was a close-knit, churchgoing community that frowned on its people flaunting their affairs for all to see. "Trina, leave it alone."

"Lordy, Althea, you deserve some happiness. I'd be the last one to cast stones at you for going after Jared Cain. I know how you hurt when Cousin Billy got killed. Know you two hadn't tasted the pleasures of the flesh, either. Billy told me, when we were talking about where y'all were going to go for your honeymoon."

"Please." Althea felt tears spill down her cheeks. Suddenly she wished she were anywhere but here. She might as well have kept her mouth shut, for all the effect her plea had on her friend.

"Don't blame you for taking your pleasure now. Wasn't normal, the way you and Billy went on for years and years, waiting to get married until you could save enough money to start your co-op."

The good manners her mom had taught her kept Althea from tossing Trina out the shop's front door—or trying, she amended when she thought about the fact that the woman probably outweighed her by at least twenty pounds.

Since bodily harm was out, Althea chose her words carefully. The last thing she wanted was to make an enemy of Trina. Still, Trina had said more already than Althea wanted to hear.

"I'm not out to 'hook' Jared Cain, as you put it. I am not going to ask for help from him to get the co-op up and running. Whether or not I'm involved with him is my business and his, and no one else's. I don't intend to listen to any more from you."

Trina's mouth gaped, and she sputtered like a kid caught telling a big fat lie. "Well, I'll be . . . I just don't want you to get hurt."

"I won't." The older woman looked so crushed, Althea couldn't stay angry. Giving Trina a quick hug, she tried to concentrate on other things than local gossip and Jared Cain.

By the time she closed the store for the day, Althea had pretty much talked herself out of asking Jared for even the smallest smidgen of help. She might pick his brain a little for ideas of how she could get her co-op underway, but she couldn't risk taking that a step further. She refused to ask him to share her dream, or help her make it come true.

When Althea got to Jim's house, he was waiting on the porch. "Sit down," he said. "We need to talk."

"Mary's all right, isn't she?"

"She's in bed, resting. The trip home tired her out, but she's doing okay. It's you I'm worried about right now."

Althea shot her brother a questioning look. He'd stopped rocking and was staring out toward the highway in front of his house, a grim look on his weathered face.

"How serious are you and Cain?" he asked.

"We're dating. Why?"

"Because people are talking about the way you two are carrying on. I hear you've spent the night at his

THE PUBLISHERS OF ZEBRA BOUQUET

are making this special offer to lovers of contemporary romances to introduce this exciting new line of novels. Zebra's Bouquet Romances have been praised by critics and authors alike as being of the highest quality and best written romantic fiction available today.

♥

EACH FULL-LENGTH NOVEL

has been written by authors you know and love as well as by up and coming writers that you'll only find with Zebra Bouquet. We'll bring y the newest novels by world famous authors like Vanessa Grant, Judy Gi Ann Josephson and award winning Suzanne Barrett and Leigh Greenwood—to name just a few. Zebra Bouquet's editors have selected only the very best and highest quality for publication under the Bouquet banner.

♥

YOU'LL BE TREATED

to glamorous settings from Carnavale in Rio, the moneyed high-powere offices of New York's Wall Street, the rugged north coast of British Columbia, and the mountains of North Carolina. Bouquet Romances use these settings to spin tales of star-crossed lovers that are sure to captivate you. These stories will keep you enthralled to the very happy end.

♥

4 FREE NOVELS
As a way to introduce you to these terrific romances, the publishers of Bouquet are offering Zebra Romance readers Four Free Bouquet novels. They are yours for the asking with no obligation to buy a single book. Read them at your leisure. We are sure that after you've read these introductory books you'll want more! (If you do not wish to receive any further Bouquet novels, simply write "cancel" on the invoice and return to us within 10 days.)

SAVE 20% WITH HOME DELIVERY
Each month you'll receive four just published Bouquet Romances. We'll ship them to you as soon as they are printed (you may even get them before the bookstores). You'll have 10 days to preview these exciting novels for Free. If you decide to keep them, you'll be billed the special preferred home subscription price of just $3.20 per book; a total of just $12.80 — that's a savings of 20% off the publisher's price. If for any reason you are not satisfied simply return the novels for full credit, no questions asked. You'll never have to purchase a minimum number of books and you may cancel your subscription at any time.

GET STARTED TODAY –
NO RISK AND NO OBLIGATION

To get your introductory gift of 4 Free Bouquet Romances fill out and mail the enclosed Free Book Certificate today. We'll ship your free selections as soon as we receive this information. Remember that you are under no obligation. This is a risk free offer from the publishers of
Zebra Bouquet Romances.

Check out our website at www.kensingtonbooks.com.

FREE BOOK CERTIFICATE

Yes! I would like to take you up on your offer. Please send me 4 Free Bouquet Romance Novels as my introductory gift. I understand that unless I tell you otherwise, I will then receive the 4 newest Bouquet novels to preview each month Free for 10 days. If I decide to keep them I'll pay the preferred home subscriber's price of just $3.20 each (a total of only $12.80) plus $1.50 for shipping and handling. That's a 20% savings off the publisher's price. I understand that I may return any shipment for full credit no questions asked and I may cancel this subscription at any time with no obligation. Regardless of what I decide to do, the 4 Free introductory novels are mine to keep as Bouquet's gift.

Name _____

Address _____ Apt. _____

City _____ State _____ Zip _____

Telephone ( ) _____

Signature _____
(If under 18, parent or guardian must sign.)   BN020A

For your convenience you may charge your shipments automatically to a Visa or MasterCard so you'll never have to worry about late payments and missing shipments. If you return any shipment we'll credit your account.
Yes, charge my credit card for my "Bouquet Romance" shipments until I tell you otherwise.
☐ Visa ☐ MasterCard
Account Number _____
Expiration Date _____
Signature _____

Orders subject to acceptance by Zebra Home Subscription Service. Terms and Prices subject to change. Offer valid in U.S. only.

If this response card is missing, call us at 1-888-345-BOOK.

Be sure to visit our website at www.kensingtonbooks.com

BOUQUET ROMANCE
120 Brighton Road
P.O. BOX 5214
Clifton, New Jersey 07015-5214

AFFIX STAMP HERE

fancy place on Big Bear Mountain. If that's true, you'd best be plannin' a wedding."

Althea squelched a sudden urge to scream. She loved her brother, but the man was more straitlaced than their preacher father had ever been. "There's not going to be a wedding. Jared and I don't have that kind of relationship."

"Are you or aren't you sleeping with the man?"

"I won't dignify that question with an answer." One lecture in one day was more than enough to suit Althea. "Where's Gracie? I need to take her and get home."

Jim stood and glared down at Althea as if he couldn't believe his ears. "I won't have you letting my little girl see you acting like white trash. Don't you go carrying on with Cain while you're takin' care of her."

Althea tried hard to control her temper. "I'd hardly carry on, as you put it, in front of a child, and you know it, Jim Simmons." If it weren't that she knew Mary needed rest and Jim considered child care women's work, Althea would have told her sanctimonious brother to take care of his daughter himself.

"Look, Althea, I just don't want you getting hurt. Cain may have been born around here, but he's spent too long in Atlanta not to have had fast city ways rub off on him. You're no match for a man like him. Plenty of good men would be proud to make you their wife. Wife, Althea, not fancy woman."

"I don't have to stand here and listen to you insult me, Jim. Do you want me to take Gracie or not?"

A shrill cry sent Jim running inside, only to come back a few seconds later with a harried look on his face and a screaming infant in his arms. "Take Gracie, please. She's got cabin fever. It's going to be all I can do to take care of Mary and little Jim. Don't be mad. I'm just looking out for you the way Ma and Pa would have wanted."

Althea nodded. She tried to keep in mind that Jim had gone through hell just last week, not knowing whether Mary was going to live or die. "I'll go see Mary and help get Gracie ready to go."

As she drove home, listening to her niece chatter about her new baby brother, Althea tried hard not to hope Jared would call.

"No, Gracie." It had been less than twenty-four hours since she'd brought her niece home, and Althea was already exhausted. She sprinted from her kitchen to the living room, arriving just in time to rescue a photo of Jim and Mary at their wedding before their daughter could manage to rip it out of its frame.

"Want Mommy. Daddy." Tears welled up in Gracie's eyes.

Althea felt like a monster, but she wished Jim would take some more time off work and take care of his family. Gracie needed him and Mary as much as Mary needed peace and quiet to recover from little Jim's birth. "Don't you like staying with me?" she asked when Gracie kept staring at her parents' picture.

"Mommy don't want me."

"Of course she does. She just needs to rest. Having a baby's hard work."

Gracie's lower lip trembled. "Hate my brother."

"Now, you know you don't. Before you know it, he'll be big enough to play with you." Althea had no idea what else she might say. Gracie obviously had been bitten by the jealous bug.

"Don't want to play with him. Want him to go away." Her expression defiant, Gracie picked up a shiny rock she'd picked up on the driveway outside and sent it crashing to the floor.

"Gracie, don't."

"I will."

How could a sweet child turn into a monster in less than a week? Althea's palm itched as she tried to make up her mind whether to pick up the phone and call for help or stick it out a while longer and see if Gracie would revert to her pre-baby self.

Compassion for her brother and sister-in-law won out. She scooped Gracie into her arms and carried her to the spare room. "Bedtime," she muttered between clenched teeth.

"No."

Althea figured she could hold out longer than Gracie could stay awake, so she wrestled the child out of her clothes and into a pink cotton nightshirt. "Look here. See Donald Duck. Mommy sent your favorite nightshirt," she said, her tone a lot brighter than her mood.

Gracie glared, said nothing. When Althea tucked her into the narrow bed and pulled a quilt up to her chin, the little girl rolled over and stared at the wall. She'd effectively shut Althea out.

She couldn't leave the little girl alone in the dark, not until she slept. Watching Gracie, feeling the insecurity only time and her loving parents could dispel, made Althea feel guilty for having let Gracie's antics get to her.

When the slowing of her breathing let Althea know Gracie had finally fallen asleep, she left her to her dreams and shuffled off to her own bed.

If she hadn't been so tired, she would have called Jared just to hear his low, sexy drawl.

FOURTEEN

Where was Althea? This was the third time he'd tried to call her since yesterday, when she'd said she had to spend the next few days taking care of her niece. Jared set down the phone and stared at the empty chair next to the quilt stand.

Lonely and bored, he went out onto the porch. A warm breeze mussed his hair and tempted him to go find a fishing pole so he could toss a line in the stream.

He missed having her here. She could bring Jim's daughter up here and let him help her entertain the little girl. For the first time in years, Jared thought of the times he and his dad had trekked through the woods. Dad had shown endless patience, answering his questions about the rocks and trees and berries and the birds and squirrels and insects that had caught his eye.

A good-sized trout leaped out of the fast-moving water of the stream, then flopped back in. Jared followed the fish downstream with his gaze. The temptation was too much. He trotted to the garage to get his tackle box and a rod and reel.

The phone rang just as he cast out a line. If he hadn't hoped it might be Althea, he'd have let the answering machine take the call. When he heard her voice, he was glad he'd come in. He lost no time, taking her up on an invitation to join her and her niece for a picnic at Lake Winfield Scott.

As Jared hosed off his fishing gear, he wondered why Althea had sounded stressed out. It had to be Jim's little girl, he guessed. What had he let himself in for just to spend time with Althea? He'd never been around a child. What did one do to entertain a three-year-old?

He went inside and started to load a couple of kids' games onto his laptop before he realized they weren't exactly age appropriate for a toddler. Instead, he loaded the pole he'd been fishing with into the trunk of his car.

If his mom had stayed on the mountain after Dad had died, Jared wouldn't have grown up not having a clue about children or families—or what this strange emotion he felt for Althea might be. But they'd moved to Atlanta, into his uncle's cold household, and Jared was what he'd become. As he drove the fifteen miles or so of winding road to Lake Winfield Scott, he hoped he'd meet with at least one girl's approval today.

"Aunt Althea, is that your friend? Why don't that car have any top?"

Althea looked in the direction Gracie's stubby finger pointed. "That's him. The car's a convertible. Its top goes up and down." To her, Jared looked impossibly handsome when he got out of the Mercedes and strode toward them, his dark hair blown by the wind.

Gracie raced around the picnic area, her short sandy ringlets bouncing, her blue eyes bright. Ordinarily she would have run out of steam by this time of day, but

Althea imagined she was running off energy she'd stored up while she stayed with Mary's older sister. Jane, an austere woman who wasn't known for putting up with childish shenanigans, had probably kept her cooped up in her cabin.

Althea sighed. Briefly she considered calling Jane to learn her secret for keeping Gracie quiet. Then Jared joined her. He gave her a quick, hard kiss.

"Jared. I'm glad you came." Her lips tingled, and she felt vibrant. Alive. "Gracie, come say hello to Mr. Cain."

"Hi, Mr. Cain," the little girl shouted without missing a beat.

"Hello, Gracie." Smiling at Gracie's antics, Jared stepped closer to Althea, gave her another kiss. "I've missed you."

"I've thought about you, too."

Oh, no, there went Gracie. "Gracie, you get back here. I told you to stay away from the road." Jared would think she had no business trying to watch her rambunctious niece, not to mention he'd probably swear off the idea of ever becoming a parent.

Not that she should care about that. They didn't have that kind of a relationship. Still, she didn't want him to think she was a pushover for the tiny tyrant. "Gracie, I said get over here."

"Want me to take her fishing?" Jared gestured toward the crystal-clear lake, where fifteen or twenty people were already casting their lines.

She should have thought of that. "That might keep her attention for a few minutes, but I didn't bring any fishing poles. Gracie!" she yelled. "If you don't stay here with us, I'm going to take you home."

He grinned. "I've got a pole in the trunk. Don't know why I brought it, except that I already had it out. I got bored with the project I was trying to finish today, and I'd just dunked a line in the stream when you called."

Why was Gracie being so obnoxious? Instead of coming back when Althea told her to, she'd headed for the parking lot. "I've got to grab her before she gets herself run over," Althea said. "If you're game, go ahead and bring out the fishing pole." Leaving him standing by the table, she took off after Gracie.

Before she could grab the willful toddler, Jared caught her. He grinned, tucked the little girl neatly under his arm, and strolled to Althea. If he minded Gracie's kicking and screaming, it didn't show. "You shouldn't run away from your aunt," he said mildly when he set her down. "Stay put. I'm going to get a pole. We're going fishing."

Gracie stopped yelling, then tilted her head back to stare up at Jared. "Go fishin'?"

"Fishing." Althea was fairly sure Jared would rather use Gracie as bait. She'd nearly come to contemplating murder herself, but she was ready to try anything to calm the child down. "You've got to do what Mr. Cain tells you."

Jared came back, pole and tackle box in hand. "Come on, Gracie. Let's see if we can catch a fish while Aunt Althea gets the picnic basket unloaded."

"Want Aunt Althea to come, too."

"She'll come as soon as she's finished here." He grabbed Gracie's hand, which gave her no choice but to scurry along beside him as he strode toward the grassy shore of the lake.

Althea tried not to feel relieved. It didn't work. What had happened to make her need Jared's help to entertain one small child? Was it his take-over manner or his quiet confidence that undermined her independence and made her feel she needed him?

Oh, well, Gracie would start giving Jared the devil's own time soon enough. When she did, Althea figured she'd regain her self-confidence. She glanced toward the lake, though, and saw Gracie holding the pole. Jared knelt behind her, steadying her small hands.

She wouldn't stare. The peace between man and toddler couldn't last. She knew her niece. Althea took a checkered tablecloth out of the oak-slat picnic basket and spread it over a wooden table shaded by two massive cedar trees.

She'd packed their lunches into three brown bags and tucked jars of sweet tea and milk into a small round cooler. When she'd set out plates, forks, and napkins that matched the tablecloth, her work was finished.

Since Jared hadn't screamed for mercy yet, Althea dug an unfinished pillow top out of her bag. Her head ached, and her body protested the rigors Gracie had put it through in the twenty hours or so that she'd been tending the little dynamo.

Sighing, she picked up her needle and began to quilt the pillow top she'd made from scraps left over from Jared's quilt. She'd made about five stitches, she guessed, before she heard Gracie yell.

"Come here, Aunt Althea. We caught a fish!"

"Let me get him off the hook. He's too little to keep." Jared sounded a lot calmer than Althea felt, but then he hadn't had to deal with Gracie for nearly a full day.

She set her quilting down and hurried to the lake. "Oh, my." A tiny trout dangled from the line, thrashing mightily as Jared set the pole down and tried to get a hold on it.

Gracie pouted. "No throw him back. I want to eat him."

Althea sensed a tantrum coming on. "Jared's right," she told Gracie, not really expecting her to listen. "He's too little. He's got to go back in the lake. Maybe you can catch him again in a few years, after he's grown up."

"No. I wanna eat him now." Hands on her hips, the little girl stuck out her lower lip.

"Sorry, Gracie." Jared gently placed the trout back in the water. "There he goes."

Althea held her breath, certain Gracie would scream, but she simply stared into the water and watched the little fish swim away. Apparently Jared had a knack for controlling people of all ages.

"Come on, let's eat," she said. "I've got our lunch ready."

"I want my fish."

They weren't off free yet. When Gracie's lower lip began to tremble, though, Jared picked her up. "Come on, I'll bet Aunt Althea's picnic is a lot better than that little fish. Let's eat." With that, he strode toward the picnic table.

Althea followed, amazed that Gracie hadn't pitched another fit. Jared obviously had made a hit with her. "The bags have your names on them," she called when they reached the table and started to sit down.

After lunch, Gracie seemed to wilt. Althea had never been so grateful for the respite as when the little girl fell asleep on a blanket under one of the towering cedars.

"She's a handful," Jared said, but his grin took the bite from the words.

That was an understatement if Althea had ever heard one. "I'm sorry to have dumped her on you like that, but thanks anyhow. Five days with Mary's sister did wonders toward turning a nice little girl into a brat."

Jared grinned. "She's cute, and no more a brat than a lot of kids."

"You've had lots of experience with children?" She wouldn't doubt it, considering the slick way he'd handled Gracie.

"I've watched a lot of them giving their mothers fits in malls. You had to be a lot like Gracie when you were her age."

Althea wouldn't dignify that accusation with a reply. "You won her over, taking her fishing," she said, changing the subject.

He grinned. "Blind luck. I had to do something or she was going to make you crazy. I had no idea she'd take to fishing the way she did. I've never been around a little one before, at least not up close and personal."

She reached across the table, patted his hand. "That's right; you're an only child. I might as well have been, since Jim was so much older."

His expression grew warm, then hot. It kindled a flame deep inside Althea. "I've missed you these last few nights," he told her, his tone like slow-flowing honey.

"I've missed you, too."

"How long will Gracie be staying with you?"

His eyes looked deep green today, their color reflecting colors of the evergreens along with the green-gold grass beneath their feet. When he looked at her, she couldn't help remembering the delicious feelings his magic touch evoked.

"Until next Wednesday. Unless I give up before that and dump Gracie back on Jim, no matter how he begs me to keep her."

"May I come visit?"

She squeezed his hand, then looked into his eyes. "I wish you would. Privacy will be in short supply, though." Briefly she recalled her brother's warning, then discounted it. She'd honor Jim's wishes and refrain from taking Gracie to Jared's place—but she'd be darned if her brother would keep her from seeing him in her own home.

He leaned across the table and whispered in her ear. "I'll let you in on a secret. It's not just the sex I'm missing, sweetheart, and that scares me half to death."

That thought stayed with Jared. It disturbed him all afternoon at the lake and throughout the next few days when he was home, taking care of business via phone and fax. Whatever it was that made him need Althea more than he needed his next meal terrified him.

It kept him here, when he should have driven to Atlanta. He could have ironed out some sticky problems a whole lot more efficiently there than he'd done via phone and fax.

He couldn't recall ever having had such powerful emotion grab him and carry him away from the practical path his mind had always taken. But she'd tied him in knots, that was for certain.

He found himself counting the days until Wednesday, when Gracie would go back home. Not able to relax because he missed her so much, he picked up the phone and dialed her number.

"May I bring burgers for you and Gracie tonight?" he asked when she answered.

A trip to Blairsville later, Jared stood on the narrow porch at Althea's cabin, fast food in hand. Waxy-leafed plants in clay pots that nearly matched the color of their small red flowers reminded him of some flowers his mom had grown when he was a boy.

He knocked, then stared at the flowers while he waited. Briefly he thought of getting some for his own porch, but he discarded the idea. He wasn't into plant genocide—and he knew damn well he'd get busy on some project, forget to water them, and let them die.

When the door opened, he turned. Althea, her hair askew, looked as though Gracie were putting her through her paces. "You okay?" he asked.

"I am now. Come on in. Jim came by fifteen minutes ago and took his little angel home. He said Mary had been missing her, although I can't imagine why. I hope you're hungry—you can eat Gracie's hamburger as well as your own."

Jared stepped inside. Althea's cabin was a riot of colors and textures. There were patchwork pillows in brilliant reds and blues and curtains made out of fragile-looking, yellowed lace. She'd put framed photos on every flat surface. Black-and-white prints faded to sepia tones sat side by side with brilliant color snapshots.

A studio portrait of a woman who looked a lot like Althea, a stern-looking man, and a boy he recognized as Jim, and a toddler caught his eye. "Your family?"

She nodded, then picked up the photo and handed it to him. "That's what I looked like when I was Gracie's age."

"You look like your mother now." Try as he might, Jared couldn't erase the picture that had come into his mind of Althea on the porch at his place, holding a toddler in her arms. A toddler who looked a lot like him.

She took the picture and set it back on the table by the couch. "We'd better eat those hamburgers before they get cold. Kitchen's this way."

Nothing was cooking, but the room still smelled of cinnamon and spice. It reminded Jared of the peach cobbler Althea had brought the night they finally made love for the first time. He sat down at the small table, then took the burgers and fries out of their wrappings.

Copper molds hung on the walls. All sizes and types of pitchers sat on shelves above the counters. Jared wolfed down his food. There must have been a story behind each of these mementoes. They must have reminded Althea of something or someone who had touched her life. When Jared pictured his own bare walls, he felt empty inside.

Althea looked exhausted. Jared got up and stood behind her chair. As he massaged her neck and shoulders, he felt her tension and hoped he could make it go away.

"That feels like heaven." She dropped her chin to her chest, then let out a sigh.

There. Her muscles were starting to relax. "Want me to give you the full treatment?"

"What's that?"

"A head-to-toe massage, guaranteed to get rid of the wearies."

"Sounds wonderful. I was never so happy to see my brother as I was today. Don't get me wrong—I love Gracie dearly, but she's a handful."

Jared laughed. He'd enjoyed the little girl a lot more than he'd expected to. "If she were picture perfect, she wouldn't be Gracie."

Althea lifted her head, then rested it against Jared's belly. "She's usually a lot better. I imagine she's finding it hard to accept that she's got competition now for Jim and Mary's attention."

That made sense. "I don't guess she wants to share them any more than I want to share you." Unfortunately, Jared wasn't three years old and throwing tantrums wasn't his style. "Come on. Lie down and I'll make you feel real good."

FIFTEEN

Althea smiled. Jared was the best medicine she could think of, better even than a good night's rest. "All right, let's go to bed."

When she opened the door to her bedroom, she spotted Bill's picture. How could she have forgotten? She looked at Jared, and choked up when she saw the hurt look in his eyes.

Quickly, she went to the nightstand beside her bed and picked up the framed photo. "I—didn't think. I'll put it away."

"It's okay. Lie down."

He sounded all right. Maybe she'd misread his feelings. Seen something that wasn't there. Still, she didn't want any painful memories between them when they made love. Ignoring his whispered instruction, she opened the drawer of the nightstand and placed Bill's photo on top of a stack of quilting magazines.

Then she turned and faced Jared. Fighting down the urge to keep herself modestly covered here in this familiar room, she peeled off her clothes one item at the time until she stood before him, naked.

She smiled when she met his gaze. "I don't think of Bill when I think of making love."

"I know." His expression softened, and his hands went to his belt.

In slow motion, he shed his shoes and socks while she lay across her bed, her heart beating with anticipation. He came down beside her, then knelt at her side.

"Roll over on your stomach," he told her.

When she did, he began gently kneading her flesh with his fingers, coaxing out the tension that had been building since her confrontation with Jim last week.

She closed her eyes and took long, cleansing breaths. For the time being she let herself go. She concentrated on the delicious feel of Jared's hands on her, and the knowledge that he stood between her and loneliness.

His touch lightened, becoming more like a lover's than a healer's. Althea sighed and turned so she could look at him. His dark eyes began to mirror the passion she felt igniting deep inside her.

He looked like a man with a purpose. Like a man who wanted her above all else. Like a man in love. When he watched her like this, she couldn't suppress the unwanted emotions that bubbled to the surface of her mind. Entranced, she gave up trying to deny her feelings. She put herself in his keeping, and trusted he would bring them both the release they sought.

"Jared."

His hands went still, heated her flesh where they touched. "What, sweetheart?"

"The way you touch me feels so good."

"I'm glad." He glanced at his big, roughened hands, dark against the pale skin of her torso. His hot gaze scorched her cheeks.

Suddenly she felt shy, lying naked and vulnerable while he sat there fully clothed. "Take off your clothes."

"Not yet." He leaned over, nuzzled her breast, then blew gently on the nipple he'd dampened with his tongue.

"Please."

"Be patient. Don't think. Feel."

Strong, agile fingers caressed her, thrilled her, made her want them everywhere. His hot, moist breath bathed her skin, made it super-sensitive to the slick abrasion of his tongue. Everywhere he touched her he created a sensual feast, even in places she'd never dreamed had erotic promise.

His silky hair beneath her fingers, the rough-soft denim of his jeans against her thighs, every sensation took her higher, made her greedy for more. The blue-rose colors of twilight that filtered through her bedroom curtains, the rich green of the forest, and the soft knit shirt he wore touched her heightened senses, took away reason.

Even the clean, faintly spicy scent of the bed linens became an aphrodisiac when it mingled with the smell of him . . . and her . . . and passion.

Each point of contact made her want more. She shifted, curled her body around him, felt his heat and hardness, and silently cursed the barrier of his clothes. But he wouldn't give in to her unspoken demands.

He took her higher, higher than she dreamed she could go, touched her everywhere but where she ached to feel his hands and mouth. Every cell in her body yearned for satisfaction.

"Please, Jared."

"Soon."

When she would have touched him, torn away his offending garments, he trapped her hands, caught them above her head with one of his, and continued his delicious torture.

Every pleasure she'd ever known and every pain she'd suffered passed before her in a montage of brilliant colors. She loved him and hated him, begged him to take her over the edge and to bring her back to earth. The fires of hell could burn no hotter. Arctic ice couldn't freeze her more.

He skimmed his hands and mouth over her heated skin again and again, his motions deliberate when she wished them frenzied, gentle when she wanted rough. The pressure inside her built slowly, so slowly, she became nothing but a mindless pit of pure sensation. When she thought she would surely die, he finally nudged her over the edge.

His smile bespoke pure male satisfaction as he stood beside the bed while she lay trembling in the wake of her climax, stripping off the garments she'd begged him to get rid of.

Sculpted musculature heightened by a sheen of sweat on skin bronzed in twilight's waning glow. Bold, blatant maleness swollen and needy, more than ready to fill the empty places in her body. Arms strong enough to hold her, a heart full enough to make hers whole.

She held out her arms, and he came into them. He came into her, strong and sure, filled her with his body as surely as he filled her heart. She shuddered, suddenly afraid of the power he held over her. Then he began to move and she gave herself over again to the rhythm. The sensation. The satisfaction only he could deliver.

Soon she joined him on his own journey to the heaven where only lovers could go.

When she came back to earth, he was sitting on the

edge of the bed. He'd opened the drawer that held Bill's picture.

"You loved him." His expression burned straight into her heart.

"Yes. We fell in love when we were twelve years old. If he hadn't died, we'd have been married now."

He ran a finger across her breast, then watched the nipple harden. Then he smiled. Green fire, like shards of emeralds, glowed in his eyes. "Sometimes, fate does strange things."

"Yes. Put the past away, Jared. I have."

"Are you sure?" He took a last look at the photo of a young man cut down before he'd lived. Then he set it in the drawer again and closed it.

He tried to put out the fire she was building in him when she stroked his chest, his belly. It was no use. He wanted her again. She was in his blood. And he was in hers.

She hadn't given herself to the fresh-faced boy who'd died. Only to him. Knowing that made him want her more.

He rolled over, pinned her beneath him, and buried himself in her to the hilt. Her arms clasped his hips, and her legs entangled with his.

He felt no urgency now, so soon after they'd made love before, only a need for them to be as close as a man and woman could get.

The bed sagged a bit under their weight. It cradled them, and he caught the scent of their lovemaking in its soft covers. When he flexed his hips, he felt her clench her inner muscles as if to hold him deep inside her. A lover's caress.

Love. She'd never said the word; yet every time she

took him into her body, he believed she must be giving him part of her heart.

It made sense. She had to love him or they wouldn't be making love. His jealousy of a dead man banished, he tightened his arms around her and buried her face in the soft crook of her neck. He stroked her with his body, slow and deep.

Later, her climax triggered his own. Keeping their bodies joined, Jared turned on his side and held Althea close. He couldn't recall ever having felt so content—so complete.

The next morning, Jared went home when Althea left to open her shop. After starting a pot of coffee, he put in a call to Harriet and pressed her to get an answer about the property he wanted to buy for Althea's co-op. It was early afternoon when she called him back.

His gaze on the unfinished quilt on its big pine stand, he listened while Harriet related a counteroffer from the owner of the property. He was glad she'd called now, before Althea got here.

Anxious to get the project underway and see Althea's eyes light up at his surprise, he very nearly accepted a price he knew was way too high. Then he told Harriet to deal not with him, but with Laura in his Atlanta office. His hard-nosed assistant wouldn't be tempted to give away the farm—she wasn't personally involved.

Jared was. More involved than he'd ever been with a woman. When she was with him, he wanted her closer. When she wasn't, he felt incomplete. Empty.

He called Laura and explained what he wanted, then told her to deal with Harriet. Although Laura sounded surprised that he wanted to fund a project so far from his home base, she assured him she'd get the best possible terms on the land. That detail taken care of, he turned his attention to the quilt.

Its colors reminded him of the woods, of fragrant spruce trees and towering pines, of the deep blue depths of the shimmering lake at the base of the mountain. The predictable pattern of light and dark prints and the precise geometric design soothed him.

He reached out and touched a corner where Althea had begun quilting the layers together. The patchwork top, a soft white filling, and the forest green backing he'd chosen would soon become a finished quilt. It was surprisingly soft. The finely woven cotton, already handled over and over by Althea's hands, felt almost like silk, yet warmer to his touch.

The quilt he'd slept under for years hadn't been this soft. When he'd begun making money with his computer games, he hadn't been able to get rid of the scratchy thing fast enough. It had been stiff, still scabby in places, even where repeated washing had worn the patches thin. Its filler hadn't been down-soft fiber like this, but an old blanket.

A down-home quilt, his mom had called it and the others she'd made from cloth flour sacks and scraps she'd salvaged from outgrown and worn-out clothes. Its backing had been a cheap bed sheet, coarse in spite of its thinness.

Althea was finally giving Jared the quilt his mom had promised him before their world fell apart. She had planned to make it block by block from remnants she'd buy as she could afford them, so she could finish the Flying Geese in time for him to give his bride.

Jared blinked back tears that threatened to spill from his eyes and embarrass him. This was just a quilt, the same pattern but not the same quilt his mom had started. Both quilts were pieces of cloth cut apart, then sewn together to make covers that would keep away winter's cold. That was all. Nothing more.

A loud knock at the front door startled Jared. He doubted it would be Althea this early. As he strode across the broad hardwood plank floor, he glanced at his watch. No. It would be two hours before she'd close up shop, and she'd said she had some things to do at home before joining him for the rest of the weekend. When he opened the door, he saw his visitor was Althea's brother Jim.

"Jim. What brings you here?"

"I wanted to thank you again for bringing Althea down to the hospital." Jim looked at the toes of his scuffed boots, then shifted his weight from one foot to the other.

"Mary and the baby are okay, I hope." Jared stepped back and motioned for the other man to come inside.

"Doing fine now. Mary gave me a hell of a scare, though. See you got yourself a quilt frame." Jim ran a finger down one side of the frame. "I missed sanding a couple of places here and there," he said. "Remind me to take care of the rough spots, next time I come over."

Jared nodded. He was beginning to feel a little uneasy about the way Althea's big brother was eyeing the quilt. Damn it, he wasn't going to . . .

Jim looked away from the quilt frame, his fists clenched. He turned to Jared. "You sleeping with Althea?" he asked, his voice deadly calm.

"Whether I am or not is between Althea and me." Suddenly Jared felt as if he were sixteen, not thirty-six.

"It's not exactly between the two of you when folks tell me they see your flashy sports car parked in front of her house at six in the morning."

Jared looked Jim in the eye. He wished he didn't feel as though he'd been caught with his pants down. "What's between us is private. Personal."

"I don't see it that way. Althea's been away to college. She got herself some fancy ideas about making things better for folks here in the mountains, but she's still one of us. And our women don't go sleeping around without bein' in love. You'd best not be taking advantage of her tender feelings."

"I care deeply for her."

"For now or for always?" Jim's fists were still clenched, but Jared noted with relief that he'd relaxed his stance.

"Seems more like for always every day." Suddenly Jared realized how close Althea had come to stealing away his heart.

"Better be. You know, our daddy was a preacher. He'll be having a fit up there in heaven if he thinks some city slicker's taking advantage of his little girl."

Jared smiled, then laid a hand on Jim's shoulder. "I'd sooner kill myself than hurt Althea. Believe me," he said, holding the other man's somber gaze. "Go on home now, and give my best wishes to your wife and baby."

"Guess I will. You take care. And remember what I said."

As if he were likely to forget. Jim's softly spoken warning rang in Jared's ears. He stood on the porch and watched the road until Jim's panel van disappeared around the bend. Twenty minutes later, he was still standing on the porch when he heard the distinctive purr of Althea's Pathfinder.

Jared seemed preoccupied tonight, Althea thought as she put the last of their dinner dishes into the dishwasher. She poured herself some more iced tea, then walked through the living room to join him on the porch.

Flying toasters marched across the screen of Jared's laptop computer to the rhythm of a catchy song. The sounds drew her gaze to the spot on the sofa where he'd left it.

Compact, obviously powerful, and apparently used only to check out the games Jared's company was planning to sell, the portable computer reminded her of the desktop system upstairs in his bedroom. It had a printer. Two of them, if memory served.

Surely it wouldn't hurt to ask Jared to make a handful of labels. She hadn't had a chance to drive to the print shop in Dahlonega.

Althea would wait and see. Right now she needed to feel Jared's arms around her. Maybe making love would remind her the bond between them was no more than powerful chemistry and delicious sensation.

SIXTEEN

"You're quiet tonight," Althea said an hour later as she pushed her needle rhythmically through the layers of Jared's quilt.

Jared looked up from the game he was testing and watched her hands move quickly as she quilted around the dark side of a square. "Your brother stopped by to see me this afternoon," he said.

She glanced at him, a surprised look on her face. "Why?"

"He wanted to warn me off. Althea, I—the last thing I'd ever want to do is hurt you in any way. He made me feel guilty . . ."

"Darn it. Why can't that man mind his own business?"

"He thinks it is his business. I probably would, too, if you were my little sister."

Althea met his gaze, her eyes flashing ice blue fire. "Jim may think I'm still a little girl, but I'm not. We haven't done a thing I didn't want to do." Her voice softened, and her expression turned dreamy. "We've done nothing I haven't enjoyed immensely. The last thing I'm in the market for is a wedding, with or without the shotgun."

She sounded okay. She even looked okay, if a little perturbed. A worse twinge of guilt than Jim had set off hit Jared when he recalled Althea had been an innocent just a few weeks ago, despite her enthusiastic participation in their lovemaking.

He pulled her up from her chair and over to the couch. Then he sat beside her and took her hand. "It wouldn't take a shotgun to get me to stand in front of a preacher with you, sweetheart. Not even a Saturday night special. If you want to get married, I'll give in without a fight."

"Heavens, no."

Her emphatic denial dented his ego, but her horrified expression smashed it to bits. "You sure know how to make a guy feel bad," he said, hoping she'd think he was teasing her.

She lifted her hand to his lips as if to silence him. "I'm just fine with us the way we are. No promises, no plans. Just us together, today and maybe tomorrow, as long as being together feels so right. And, Jared, it does feel right. Very right. I love the way you make love with me."

That was something. Maybe not all he'd hoped for, but enough to hold onto for the time being. Jared drew Althea into his arms and shut down his mind. He gave his body free rein, and delivered on the only promise she seemed willing to take from him.

When he woke up the next morning and found Althea's side of the bed empty, Jared looked around. There she was, checking out the computer on his desk.

She made his plain white shirt look sexy, he noticed

as he padded across the room. While she stared at the psychedelic screen saver undulating on the monitor, he stood behind her, hands on her shoulders.

"Go on," he said. "Wiggle the mouse. It won't bite you. I promise."

Her shoulders tensed beneath his fingers. "I have seen a computer before, Jared. I've even used one."

"Then do me a favor. Take a look at this game, and let me know what you think. Its name has to go, but otherwise I think it'll be a winner." He leaned over her and tapped the mouse. When the screen saver disappeared, a scowling pirate's face appeared.

She reached up to her shoulders and covered his hands with hers. "Sorry. I'm not at my best in the mornings. What's the object of this game?"

"To see how much you can get of the buccaneer's treasure."

"Who is he?" She inclined her head toward the monitor.

"He's Captain Morgan now, but that's going to change. I can't go selling games to kids if their names remind their parents of rum."

"Oh."

She made no move to begin the game, so he moved the mouse and clicked the button a few times. "There, you've found the gold chest. Now try to get through the maze and knock off each one of the doubloons."

She found and captured a couple of the brightly colored disks, then took her hand off the mouse. "Jared, I'm not much into games."

Something was bothering her. She'd acted peculiar last night, and now she was acting as if he'd asked her to walk over coals. Leaning over, he shut off Captain

Morgan, then took hold of the swivel chair where she was sitting and turned her around to face him. "Tell me what's wrong."

"Nothing."

Nothing, hell. She'd shut down tighter than a fresh oyster in its shell, and he wasn't about to leave it alone. "Althea," he said, shuddering at the cold feeling he got from her shuttered gaze.

"It has nothing to do with us. I'm just tired. Worried. A little frustrated. That's all. I'll work it out."

He stroked her cheek. "Maybe I could help."

"No. It's my problem. My project. It has nothing to do with you."

Her project. The co-op? Jared started to tell Althea what he planned to do, then changed his mind. Instead he pulled her into his arms and held her as gently as if she were a child. For a long time they stood by the computer, until he felt the tension in her muscles ease.

When she spoke, her words were muffled against his chest. Her breath tickled him, but he couldn't make out what she'd said. "What did you say, sweetheart?"

She hesitated, as if she felt whatever it was that she needed would be too much to request. "Would you let me make a few labels for Trina's jelly jars on one of your computers?" she finally asked.

Was that all that was bothering her? "Sure. What size does she want?" He opened a file cabinet and read off the dimensions of the laser labels he had on hand.

She picked the size he used to label floppy disks, but shook her head when he tried to hand her an unopened box of the labels. "I only need to make enough for the jars she puts out for sale before school opens next month. I can make her more when I can get to the computer there."

"Feel free. Use whatever you need. What program do you usually use to make them?"

She named a well-known word processing program, one he was surprised she hadn't recognized from its distinctive icon on the desktop.

Bending over, he clicked on the icon and brought the program up on the screen. "There it is, sweetheart. Do your thing."

She looked confused. "This doesn't look familiar."

"It's the newest version. I'll show you."

With a few clicks of the mouse, he formatted the labels. "There. Type in whatever you want on them." When she finished, he showed her how to add a border and decorate the labels with clip art from the software's basic library.

"Thank you." She looked at the three pages of labels, then shook her head when Jared offered to make some more. "I wouldn't have asked to do these, but Trina has such awful handwriting."

At first Jared didn't see the connection between asking to use his computer and Trina's penmanship, but then he realized the issue wasn't labels. It was pride. Althea salvaged Trina's pride by getting her the labels, but she compromised her own by asking him for help.

Jared wondered if his plan to make Althea's dream for a co-op come true would thrill her as much as he'd first thought it would. He had a feeling her prickly pride might get in the way.

***

A little later, Althea stood in her shop, staring at the brightly colored labels Jared had helped her make. Paper. That was all they were. She shouldn't look at them and see another erosion of her hard-won independence.

She'd been her parents' daughter; Bill's girlfriend first, then his fiancée. First as a child, then as a woman, Althea had leaned on others until, one by one, they'd died. The losses had left her empty and shattered her life's direction. How terribly she had hurt. When the worst of the pain finally faded, she'd sworn to depend only on herself, to maintain her independence at all costs.

Now Jim was acting like the enraged father of a teenager, and Jared was unwittingly undermining her resolve not to rely on others. Althea shook her head, then started to rearrange bolts of fabric on a shelf.

She couldn't forget the lessons she'd learned so painfully. She couldn't risk history repeating itself.

Her anger bubbled over, threatened to explode until she tamped it down. Jim had no business butting into her life as though he thought she was eighteen years old and none too bright. But she'd deal with him later.

Tires crunched on the gravel outside. Althea looked out the window. Trina had her arms full. Quickly, Althea went to help her. "I've got the door. Come on in."

Trina smiled. "You get the first dozen jars. Did you make the labels?"

"They're on the counter. I think you'll like them." Althea opened the carton and held a clear glass jar of garnet-toned jelly up to the light.

"My. Gettin' fancy, aren't you?" Trina grinned from ear to ear as she separated labels from their backing before fastening them to the jars of jelly. "Color and all. The blackberry bush in the background adds a nice touch."

"Thank Jared. He's got the latest thing in programs, and a color printer, too." Althea would have felt a lot better if she'd been able to do the labels, even simple black-and-white ones, without asking for anybody's help.

"I will, if I ever run into him. You tell him for me."

"All right."

Trina looked at her jelly, then at the rest of the labels. "I'd better go. I've got eight dozen more jars out in the truck. I promised Maude over at Uncle Ed's General Store that I'd bring them today. I need to hurry because when I get home, I've got to start another batch. Berries are real plentiful this year. Me and the boys picked almost five gallons yesterday."

When she thought about picking blackberries, Althea could practically feel their evil spines dig into her flesh. Unfortunately, the idea of eating fresh blackberry cobbler made her mouth water and overwhelmed her reluctance to put her hide in jeopardy to get the main ingredient. "I may go pick a few myself."

"Get your man to help. There used to be plenty of blackberry thickets up on Big Bear Mountain. Tempt him with a pie, or maybe some fresh blackberries with homemade ice cream."

"I just might. You have a good day, now." Suddenly Althea's interest in fixing a high-calorie treat made with berries turned into a craving. Maybe, after she had it out with her meddling brother, she'd see if Jared was up for battling the berry brambles with her. Good thing it didn't get dark much before nine o'clock.

COMING HOME

***

At five, Althea closed the shop and headed for Jim's. When she pulled into the driveway behind her brother's truck, she noticed Mary and the baby on the old-fashioned swing Jim had hooked into the ceiling of the porch.

"How's my new nephew?" she asked as she climbed the steps.

Mary smiled. "He's precious."

"That he is." The baby looked fine, tiny but healthy. "How are you feeling?"

"Tired." She leaned down and brushed a kiss across her son's downy head. "Happy, though."

"Where's Jim?"

"Taking a walk with Gracie. She wore me out today."

Althea didn't doubt that. "When will they be back?" Now that she was here, she wanted to get the confrontation over with.

Mary shrugged. "Soon, I guess. Jim always wants his supper before six o'clock. I'd better go in and get it ready. You're welcome to join us."

Her expression pained, she got up. Moving very slowly, she set the baby in a cradle in the living room as they walked through the house toward the kitchen.

To Althea's way of thinking, Mary looked as though she should be in bed, not standing up and fixing meals for Jim. She looked around the small kitchen. "What can I do to help?"

"Nothing. Everything's ready but the biscuits."

When Mary bent to put the pan in the oven, her round face turned pale and she began to tremble.

"Are you all right?" Althea asked, hurrying to her and steadying her as best she could.

Mary sank onto a chair and sighed. "I'm getting there. Still can't do much, though."

"You shouldn't be trying to cook yet." The woman had had a cesarean section less than three weeks ago, not to mention the stroke that had precipitated it or the high blood pressure that apparently had caused the stroke. Althea doubted many people would expect Mary to do any work at all. "Surely Jim can manage to fix a few meals."

"He did, up until a few days ago. I'll be okay." Mary sounded more confident about that than Althea felt.

"At least let me set the table for you."

"All right. You know where the dishes are. You are going to stay for supper, aren't you?"

"I don't think so." Althea doubted she'd be welcome after saying what she intended to say to her meddlesome brother.

Just then Jim stepped through the back door, Gracie on his shoulders. "Jim, I need to have a few words with you," Althea said.

Jim met Althea's gaze. As he set his daughter down, he managed an intimidating scowl. "Gracie, you run to your room now."

"Don't want to."

Mary looked puzzled when she turned to her little girl. "Do as your daddy says, sweetie."

Gracie's lower lip trembled, the way Althea had noticed it always did before she burst into tears. "Do I have to?" she asked.

"Yes, you do. Go on now. Play with your dollies until suppertime." Patting Gracie on her blond head,

Mary gently shooed her out of the room. Then she turned to Jim. "What are you going to say that Gracie shouldn't hear?"

"This. My sister's making a fool of herself with Jared Cain." He pulled out a straight chair and straddled it. "I guess that's what you want to talk about," he said when he looked Althea in the eye.

"I want to talk about you meddling into what should be between me and Jared. About you threatening Jared. Darn it, Jim, you might as well have stuck both barrels of a shotgun in his face."

"More than one person's told me they saw Cain's fancy sports car in front of your cabin late one night. That they've driven by other nights and noticed your car wasn't there. If you wanted your sinnin' to stay between the two of you, you should have been more careful to make things look right."

Althea wanted to scream, but she held onto her temper. Why couldn't folks mind their own business? "You want to listen to gossip, go right ahead. The point is, you're my brother, not my keeper. You've got no right judging . . ."

"I've got every right. Ma and Pa expected me to look after you 'til you got married. Never thought I'd have to say my own sister was acting like a loose woman." Jim looked mad enough to chew nails.

"I'm no loose woman. Jared's the only man I've ever . . . What I mean is, he's . . ."

"It just takes one, sister. Don't you remember what Ma used to tell us?"

When had her brother turned into such a sanctimonious prude? "I suppose you stayed pure as the snow on the mountaintops in winter 'til you married Mary."

Jim had the decency to turn red in the face. Apparently he'd spotted something interesting on the linoleum floor, judging from the way he kept looking at it. Finally he shot Althea a disgusted look. "I'm a man, damn it. We're talking about you."

"No, we aren't. Not anymore. Jim, you leave Jared alone—and keep your nose out of my business."

"What happens when you get pregnant? Ever think about that? About bringing up a kid with no pa?"

Althea refused to dignify that question with a reply.

Jim stood, a fierce expression on his face. "I've said it all, girl. Either you marry that city slicker or you stop sinnin' with him. You're making me ashamed to be your brother." He slammed a meaty fist onto the tabletop.

"Jim, calm down." Mary laid a work-roughened hand on his, then turned to Althea. "He means well, you know. He's just . . ."

"I'm tired of hearing from half the folks who live in these mountains that my sister's behaving like a slut." Jim shook off Mary's hand before starting to pace back and forth across the worn floor.

Mary moved in front of him. That stopped him, made him look her in the eye. "We didn't wait 'til our wedding night," she said softly. "Do you think I'm a loose woman?"

"Mary, be quiet. This isn't about us."

Hands on her ample hips, Mary held her ground. "Well, we did the exact same thing that you're having a tizzy fit over Althea doin'."

"She's right, Jim." Determined not to show her brother how much his opinion stung her, Althea choked back her tears.

Jim faced down his wife. "It's not the same. We didn't flaunt it for everybody to see. And we didn't sleep together until we knew we were getting married."

"Maybe Althea doesn't want to get married. Did you ever think of that?" Though she spoke softly, Mary's tone commanded attention.

"Every woman wants to get married."

Althea looked Jim in the eye. "I don't. Did you ever think that losing Bill might have made me realize it hurts too much when you love somebody? I've got the right to enjoy a man without tying myself to him for life, no matter what you say."

"So that's what you're doing? Enjoying Jared Cain?" *Enjoying* came out of Jim's mouth sounding like an indictment.

"As I said before, it's not your concern. And don't you dare go talking to Jared again about our relationship."

Heartsick, Althea moved toward the door. "I'm sorry you don't like the way I'm living, but it's my life. Be seeing you." With that, she turned away.

By the time she got to Jared's place, she couldn't hold back her tears.

SEVENTEEN

If there were anything Jared hated, it was seeing Althea cry. He stepped onto the porch and pulled her into a loose embrace. "What's wrong, sweetheart?"

"Jim." She buried her face against his shoulder. "I'm so mad at him, I could scream."

He patted her back, wishing to hell she'd stop trembling. He had no clue what might help her to feel better. "Althea, it can't be bad enough to cry over," he said, but she only sobbed harder.

Maybe if he could get her to explain . . . "What did Jim do that's got you so upset?"

"He called me a loose woman because I don't want to fall in love and get married."

"You're no loose woman, Althea." Having one lover in twenty-seven years wouldn't mark a woman as loose even by the strict standards here in the mountains. By Atlanta's more liberal code, Jared figured Althea would qualify for sainthood.

Her arms tightened around his waist. "Jim won't understand I couldn't take it if I fell in love with you, then lost you the way I lost Bill."

So that was why she worked so hard to keep their relationship strictly physical. Keeping one hand on her shoulder, Jared took a step back, then lifted her chin until she met his gaze with teary eyes.

"Why do you think you'd lose me, sweetheart?"

"I—I've lost everybody I ever loved. My folks, then Bill."

He stroked a tear off her cheek. "Do you think I'd run out on you? Don't you know me better than that?"

"I don't think you'd go on purpose. I still might lose you."

"And you might not." He took her hand. "Look at me, honey. I'm not a cop, and I don't do anything that's likely to put me in front of a criminal's gun. Chances are, I'll live to a ripe old age and die in my bed."

The hopeful look on her face made him choke up. She might not want to have tender feelings for him, but she did. They showed in the way she looked at him, the way she reached up and touched his cheek.

"If only we could see into the future—"

"Life wouldn't be much fun without its little surprises, sweetheart."

She smiled, then brushed at the damp spots her tears had made on his shirt. "Sorry about that."

"Think nothing of it. Let's go inside and see if we can forget about your run-in with your brother."

While she sat at the kitchen table, he bathed her tear-streaked cheeks with a warm, damp towel.

"Do you like blackberries?" she asked as he set the towel in the sink.

Better blackberries than tears. "Sure. Why?"

"If we can find some to pick, I'll make us a cobbler. Trina said they're plentiful this year. By the way, she said to tell you thanks for making the labels."

"Tell Trina she's welcome. She's right about there

being a lot of berries." Just yesterday, he'd spotted a huge bramble a hundred yards or so up the mountainside, so full of berries that some of the branches nearly dragged the ground. "Come on. I know where to find some. We've got maybe an hour to pick them before it gets dark."

Metal pots in one hand, he led the way to the berries. "There they are," he said when they rounded a bend in the path.

Althea seemed as happy when he handed her a cooking pot as Marcie had been when he gave her the diamond tennis bracelet he'd asked Laura to pick out for her birthday last year. Maybe he'd managed to calm her fears about getting involved. He hoped so.

As eager as a kid, he grabbed a berry-laden cane and reached for the biggest ripe blackberry.

"Ouch, damn it." He'd forgotten about the thorns. "Watch out, sweetheart. These things stick."

She dropped a handful of berries into her container, then reached carefully for more. "I know."

"Mom used to send me blackberry picking. I'd forgotten how scratched up I got. Somehow it made the berries sweeter." He picked a berry, plopped it into his mouth, and savored the tart-sweet taste.

She laughed. "You won't have any to take home if you keep eating them, my mom used to say. Ow."

When she stepped back, Jared noticed a cane had attached itself to one leg of her thin slacks. "Hold on. I'll get it loose."

It was more easily said than done. Every time Jared got one thorn untangled, another managed to embed itself in Althea's pants leg. Finally he freed her, but not before she suffered several more sharp pricks.

"Stay back, sweetheart. You're going to look like a pincushion if you don't. I'll pick the rest."

"You'll get scratched, too."

He kissed her nose, then grinned. "I'll be careful." No sooner had he picked up his half-filled container and turned back to the berry patch than she joined him, as if she hadn't heard a word he'd said.

"You don't obey very well." He couldn't get mad, though. The determined look on her face made him want to hug her.

When she dropped a berry into her nearly full pot, she shot him an impish smile. "No, I don't. Fill up your pan now. I can hardly wait to eat a big bowl of these berries."

Wild blackberries, sumptuous and sweet, promised to be well worth the scrapes and the puncture wounds their spiny canes inflicted in the harvesting process. Jared had the feeling that if he could ever get past Althea's prickly defenses, he'd find her love was sweeter, and infinitely more satisfying than the physical fulfillment she gave him so freely.

When he finished filling his pot, he backed away from the bramble, stopped on the path beside Althea. "I can't wait, either," he told her.

By the time they'd cleaned the berries, night was settling in, turning the sky dusky purple against the backdrop of a distant mountain framed in Jared's kitchen window.

"Let's go sit on the porch," he said after they'd scooped some ice cream and covered it with glistening berries.

Althea followed him outside. As comfortable together as if they'd been together for years, not just days, they sat on two of the oak-slat rockers and ate their treat.

Like their lovemaking, the dessert was sinfully sweet. Irresistible. Like Jared himself. He looked good enough to eat, cast in twilight shadow while the sun disappeared beyond the horizon.

She could love him so easily, if only she could control her fears. Each day she found it harder to persuade herself her emotions weren't involved. The pull Jared exerted on her was much more than lust.

His tongue darted out and captured a drop of ice cream off his upper lip.

"Taste good to you?" she asked.

"Delicious. Worth every scratch."

If she freed the stranglehold on her emotions, if she could let herself love him, would the pleasure be worth the pain of losing him?

"Althea?"

"Yes." If only she were as certain about Jared as she was about the berries. "I'll be right back," she told him when she took his bowl.

The few seconds she took to take the dishes inside gave her a chance to calm her racing heart. She sat down again, then took his hand and traced the calluses on his palm.

"I'm sorry you argued with Jim. I've been away from here so long, I didn't give a thought to folks thinking badly . . ."

"Stop, Jared. I don't care what anybody thinks. As long as we want to be together, nothing else matters." Suddenly she realized she no longer had a choice. What they shared was more than physical. A lot more. More than she had the courage to face.

He squeezed her hand, then got up and moved close to the railing. Beyond him, a silvery moon lit the blackness of the sky. The howls from some nocturnal mountain creature sent chills up her spine, made her seek the safety of Jared's strong arms.

She joined him at the porch rail. A sudden breeze ruffled his hair and caught the scent of evergreens she'd always associate with magical nights on Big Bear Mountain. With him.

He rested a hand at her waist. "I've never wanted to be with a woman before, not the way I want you."

"Let's go inside."

More than anything, Althea needed to feel his strong arms around her and hear the steady cadence of his breathing. It didn't matter if they made love. She wanted to hold him, savor the nearness of him. Tonight she'd deal with that. Her fears, she'd save for tomorrow.

Waking up with Althea in his arms was a dream come true, and the sex they shared was the best he'd ever had. But Jared wanted more. He wanted her to love him for a lifetime, not just for a little while.

He shifted her in his arms and craned his neck so he could read the clock. Three-thirty. If he hadn't gone to sleep by now, he figured he wasn't likely to nod off before the clock struck six.

Carefully, so as not to wake Althea, he untangled their bodies, slipped out of bed, and made his way to the shower. He turned the water on full blast and stepped under the needle-sharp spray.

He breathed deeply as he let the hot water do its job on muscles he hadn't realized were tense until they began to relax. Eyes closed, he reached for the soap and started to rub it over his body.

He didn't want to leave, not now, when he thought Althea was beginning to open up to him. He had to, though. Cain Software needed a marketing director, and there was no way he could hire one from here.

With a little luck, he wouldn't have to spend more than a few days in Atlanta.

Jared ducked his head under the water, then reached for the shampoo and worked up a lather.

A cool breeze hit his spine when the shower door opened. He turned, saw Althea before shampoo got in his eyes and made him blink. "Ouch."

"I startled you. I'm sorry."

"I'm sorry I woke you up." He wasn't, not really. Her sleepy voice got him instantly hard, made him yearn to bury himself inside her. Stake his claim in the most basic way it could be done.

"Let me love you, Jared."

If only she did love him.

Her mouth was velvet-smooth, and she tasted faintly like the berries they'd picked when her tongue fenced coyly with his. She slid her hands over his back while she held him tight, so tight that he could feel her nipples pressing against his chest.

Then she broke the kiss and slid down his body until she was on her knees. Her nipples grazed spots just above his knees that he hadn't realized were sensitive until now.

Inch by inch, she took him in her mouth, made him

feel ten feet tall and weak as a baby, all at the same time.

He leaned against the shower wall, not certain he could keep standing on his own when she cupped his buttocks in her hand. The way she held him to her, as though she thought he might attempt escape—a ludicrous idea, for sure—made him shudder.

She moved on him, took him deeper, then let up, her tongue swirling over him as if he were some gourmet treat. Jared closed his eyes, tried to think of Latin conjugations—computer operating systems—nuclear physics. Anything but what she was doing to him with her lips and tongue and teeth.

He was going to explode. "No more."

She didn't stop until he reached down, lifted her onto her feet, and turned her to face the built-in shower seat. With his foot, he nudged her feet wide apart.

"Bend over and hold onto the seat." The voice he heard didn't sound at all like his own.

The sight of her waiting for him like that, legs spread wide and her backside in the air, nearly made him come. Her head was bent, as if in supplication.

He took one step forward, flexed his knees, and sank himself deep inside her. He wrapped both arms around her, one high so he could fondle her breasts, the other low to hold her steady for his rhythmic thrusts. Never before had he even imagined feeling such sexual power.

Hot water sluiced over his back. Her welcoming cavern was hotter, wetter. He didn't want it to end. Not yet. She felt too good, too right. Too *his*. He gritted his teeth, deliberately bit his own tongue. Anything to distract his body from its goal, to prolong this—this feeling of power and possession.

What Althea had begun when she joined him in the shower, Jared was about to finish. In her position she was helpless to his passion, a prisoner to his will. Everywhere they touched, she burned. God help her, she loved his mastery.

She could see his hands on her breasts and at the apex of her thighs, catch glimpses of him as he thrust into her. The ragged sound of their breathing mingled like an erotic symphony.

His early-morning beard scraped sensually against her neck, reminded her that that, too, was an erotic place when he stimulated it so capably. His hot breath smelled of mint, reminded her how she loved to taste his mouth . . . his hard, fit body.

She couldn't move. She didn't care. It was enough that she saw, felt, heard, smelled, tasted. Enough for her to experience the heady elixir of being possessed.

His breathing, already ragged, turned to desperate gasps for air. He clasped her so close, she could feel his muscles contract. He pulled out, then made one final thrust.

She came as he did, gasping, grasping, seeking more than just release. Then she rested her head against the shower wall.

"Are you okay?" Very gently, Jared pulled away from her, keeping his hands on her as though he thought she might collapse.

"Yes." She wanted to look at him, verify in her mind that the fierce lover who had just possessed her so completely was the same gentle man she had joined in the shower half an hour earlier. She needed reassurance that he hadn't stolen her soul and left her an empty shell to do his bidding.

When she turned around, he was shutting off the water, as though nothing earthshaking had happened.

The heated look on his face when he suggested they go back to bed told her a very different story.

"I've got to go to Atlanta for a few days, interview candidates for a marketing director. Want to join me?" Jared asked the next morning while they ate sugared blackberries with their toast and coffee.

"I can't. I've got the shop to look after."

"Couldn't you ask Trina to come in?"

Althea shook her head. "Not while the blackberries are so plentiful. Besides, I can't afford to take off every time I get the notion."

Jared looked disappointed, but then he smiled. "That's okay. Knowing you're here will make me hurry, do what I have to do so I can get back here sooner. Want me to bring you something special?"

You.

"I can't think of anything. Except—would it be all right if I stay here so I can work on your quilt in the evenings while you're away?" If she didn't put in some time on the quilt when Jared wasn't around to distract her, it wouldn't get finished for years. And Althea did want to see him tangled up in it, looking at her as if she had hung the moon.

"I'd like knowing you're here. Waiting for me." He sounded as if he were teasing, but the expression in his dark eyes hinted he meant every word. "Come here."

When he held her, he made her feel whole. He made her want more than she feared. After she headed down the mountain, keys to his house in hand, terror began to set in.

EIGHTEEN

"What have I done?"

Long after she should have opened the shop, Althea stood in the bedroom of her cabin. She tried in vain to persuade herself she hadn't fallen in love with Jared Cain.

Desperate, she pulled Bill's picture from the drawer where she'd left it, then clutched it to her chest. She made herself relive the day she'd lost him forever, and cringed at the tearing grief that remained deep in her soul.

She probably wouldn't lose Jared the same way she'd lost Bill. He wasn't a cop, and he didn't have the kind of job that made it likely he'd ever step in front of a criminal's gun. She couldn't dispute his logic about that.

She set Bill's picture back in the drawer, then pushed the drawer shut. Funny, Jared had only spent one night here, but she felt his presence in her room as much as at his place.

She might as well face the truth. She'd done what she'd promised herself she'd never do again. She'd fallen in love and made herself vulnerable to more agony, more heartache, more pain.

Because, while Jared probably wouldn't fall victim

to a criminal's gun and he might easily outlive her, she could lose him in other ways. To the city . . . his company . . . the world he lived in. A world where she didn't belong. She had the feeling losing him that way would hurt as much as if he died. Maybe more.

"Morning, Jared."

"Welcome back."

Jared grinned as he exchanged greetings with a dozen programmers while taking a shortcut through the large open office where they worked. He allowed himself a twinge of regret that he no longer had time to come up with new games or play with ideas instead of sales projections and financial statements. "Got any new ideas on the burners?" he asked chief programmer Todd Gray.

"Always." Todd mentioned a couple of projects, then asked about his pet game. "What's going on with Captain Morgan?"

"He's scheduled to make his appearance in time for the Christmas rush—after marketing changes his name."

Todd shrugged. "I liked Captain Morgan."

"Apparently the people who named the rum did, too." The packaging for the new game was only one of many reasons Jared had to find a new marketing director—quickly.

"You staying around awhile, boss?"

"A few days. I'm going to be tied up, interviewing candidates for Marcie's job. E-mail me any prototypes you're ready for me to look at." Jared headed for his own office at the back of the building.

Laura had laid out résumés in the order the candidates were scheduled to appear for interviews. Only one applicant came from within Cain Software—a young woman Marcie had hired last year. Georgette Boyer.

A mug of steaming coffee sat on the other side of his desk next to a warm bran muffin. Laura apparently thought he needed fortification. Jared wolfed down the food, then blew on the coffee. He glanced at the clock. Five minutes before the first applicant would arrive.

By late afternoon he'd interviewed ten applicants, listened to ten hotshot ideas about how to market the quest game Todd wanted to call *Captain Morgan*. Finally finished with interviews, Jared rubbed his head as he tried to make sense of scribbles he'd made on a legal pad. When Laura came in, he glanced up from his notes.

"Any good candidates?" she asked, gesturing toward the stack of résumés on the corner of his desk.

"Boyer. I like her. Why didn't she apply for the director's job as soon as Marcie left?"

Laura shrugged. "Who knows? Maybe she was leery about trying to fill Marcie's shoes. She is short on experience."

"How much should we pay her?" Jared flipped through Boyer's presentation folder, then passed it over to Laura.

After looking through the folder, she smiled. "You've made up your mind to promote her, then?"

"Yeah. It's good for morale to promote from within. Besides, I want to get this done so I can go home." To Althea, he thought, savoring a memory of her standing on his porch, a gentle wind mussing up her hair.

Laura handed him the folder. "Start her at sixty thousand."

Surprised, he met her gaze. "Marcie made three times that much."

"When she left, she did. She didn't when she started."

"All right. Set Georgette up on an incentive program, though. I don't want to exploit an employee just because she's inexperienced."

Laura smiled. "You'd give away the place if I didn't watch you."

"I know. You tell me often enough." He recalled the special project he'd given her last week. "How's the negotiation coming for that property outside Blairsville?"

"I got a counteroffer today." She named a figure that was close to twenty thousand dollars less than he'd been prepared to pay. "The owner's willing to give a credit for the cost of grading the site and tearing out the old concrete."

He nodded. By turning over the negotiation to Laura, he'd saved himself a bundle. "Go ahead, accept the offer. My architect's cleaning up some rough plans I sketched out for the building. I'll have him fax the specs to you so you can put out a request for bids from contractors."

"How should the land be titled?" She flipped a page in the pad where she was taking notes, then glanced at Jared.

"Call Russ. I asked him last week to start the paperwork to set up a charitable foundation." He had no doubt the lawyer and his accounting manager had determined the best way to write off the costs Cain Software would incur on behalf of the co-op.

Laura scribbled another note on her pad. Then she looked him in the eye. As if she weren't sure she should say anything, she hesitated. "Jared, you need to spend more time here. Todd and the others get nervous when you're gone too long," she finally blurted out.

"Why?"

"You know how rumors go. When you stay away for weeks at the time, people start thinking you might sell out."

"Sell out? As in, to one of the big software companies?" While Jared had a couple of standing offers to do just that, he'd never given the idea of selling serious consideration. "Everybody knows I wouldn't do that."

"Do they? You've spent all summer at that mountain cabin of yours. Before that, you walked around for months as though you didn't know what was going on. At first, we thought you were missing Marcie—"

"It was never Marcie. I didn't want her to resign, of course, but personally we weren't right for each other." He looked at Laura. He'd never realized she—or anyone else who worked with him, for that matter—worried about his love life or the lack thereof.

"But you've stayed away since you broke up with her, as if it hurt too much to be here."

Standing, he picked up a letter opener and shifted it from hand to hand. "I've spent most of my life in Atlanta, Laura. I like the city and these offices. I've nothing but good thoughts about this company, and the people who've helped me make it a success."

"Then why? Why hole up in the middle of nowhere? Why make us all wonder if you're ever coming home?"

Was that what everyone thought he was doing? "The middle of nowhere, as you call it, is less than three hours away. I've been in touch every day, as much so as if I were sitting at this desk."

She reached out and touched his hand. "Tell your employees, then. Don't let them worry. They expect to see you every now and then."

Damn. He'd hoped to do the board meeting tomorrow, then head home to Althea as soon as it adjourned. No such luck. "Set a meeting for day after tomorrow. I'll see what I can do to dispel whatever crazy ideas the troops may have gotten into their heads."

"For everyone, or just the programming staff?"

"Everybody. Thanks." He made a mental note to call accounting and have them add a good-sized bonus to Laura's next paycheck. Replacing Marcie had been easy, compared to what he imagined he'd have to go through if Laura should ever decide to quit.

When she left, he glanced at his watch. Six-thirty. He picked up the phone and punched in the number for his place on Big Bear Mountain. Already he missed Althea, and he'd been away from her less than twelve hours. He pictured her the way she'd looked last night, sitting by the fireplace as she worked on his quilt. Their quilt.

"Answer the phone, sweetheart," he said when the phone rang for the third time. She had to be there. That's where she belonged. Her presence was what made his house a home.

When he heard her voice, his tension eased. It felt good to hear her, to know she'd come straight there from her shop. He explained how he'd spent his day and let her know how much he wished they were together. "I should be home day after tomorrow," he told her before they hung up.

He'd had his Althea fix, he thought as he stared at the silent phone. The fact that he'd let one woman matter so much in such a short time amazed him. It should have also scared him half to death, but it didn't. Caring for Althea felt good. Really good.

He picked up a blank legal pad and jotted down notes as they came to mind. He'd spend another hour here, then grab a pizza or something to eat at his condo. He pictured Althea there. Did her sweet scent still linger in the air, and on the pillow where she had laid her head?

A few minutes later, Jared set the paper down and slid his chair back. He could work just as well at the condo as here. When he strode out of his office, he felt good. Lonely, but very good indeed.

Stitch after tiny stitch, Althea made her needle fly around the solid and patterned rectangles within a square motif. Unlike the piecing process, quilting occupied only her hands, not her mind. She had plenty of time to listen to the tick of a big Seth Thomas clock, wonder what kind of creature outside kept making that plaintive, shrieking sound, as if he'd lost his mate.

An hour after his call, Jared's voice still echoed in her mind. She rethreaded her needle and began quilting around another square.

What would he look like in his office as he prepared a speech for the Atlanta bankers and businessmen who served on his board of directors? Was that office as devoid of personal mementoes as the condo he called home? Would his assistant, the one who'd ordered the clothes he bought her, still be there helping him?

She imagined him wearing a suit and tie, impressing a roomful of movers and shakers who sat around a massive conference table. The contrast between that image and the one she knew, of Jared in jeans or khakis and a polo shirt that echoed the colors in his quilt, made her set down her needle.

The gentle man with nothing more important on his mind than picking blackberries, watching and listening to the stream roar down Big Bear Mountain—loving her through the night—that was her illusion of Jared. The illusion she loved.

That wasn't the real man. It couldn't be. No simple dreamer, the man who had built a company from the ground up and achieved a level of success beyond simple hill folks' wildest dreams.

The realization she'd first had this morning slammed into her again. Jared Cain was way, way out of her league. She knew it, and sooner or later he would realize it, too.

When he did, she'd lose the second man she'd ever loved. Dread filled her, made her chill in spite of the warm summer night.

He needed the peace of the mountains now, but he'd tire of slow-paced living all too soon. When he did, he'd leave. He'd go back to his world, where there was no room for a simple quilt-maker whose wildest dream was to help mountain women like herself succeed by using simple skills they'd learned at their mothers' knees. No room for her.

Blinking back tears, Althea turned to her quilting. She concentrated on keeping the stitches small and even. Control. She'd control what she could, and try not to worry about the things she couldn't.

Part of her wanted to run as fast as she could, away from Jared and Big Bear Mountain, before love for him consumed her. But her heart told her it was already much too late for retreat.

The other part of her—the earthy, sensuous part she hadn't discovered until she met him—wanted to rejoice in loving him body and soul. She yearned to explore every sensual avenue lovers could travel on their journey to the stars. To live for today, and let tomorrow take care of itself.

NINETEEN

The board meeting went well—and a lot faster than Jared had hoped. He glanced at his watch after the board members left. Three o'clock.

He stared out the window and watched Ben Trainor's fire-engine-red Porsche roll out of the parking lot. He'd always thought the flashy sports car a weird choice for the portly banker who'd sat on the board since the beginning, and risked giving Jared his first loan.

He could nose around in marketing, or try his hand at designing a new game. Nothing appealed. What he wanted was Althea—here, not miles away over mountainous roads.

"Jared?"

He turned toward the sound of Laura's voice and found her standing in the doorway. "You need something?"

She smiled. "Not really. I thought you might, though. You haven't said a word since you adjourned the meeting."

He shrugged. "Nothing to say."

"You miss her."

"Who?"

"You tell me." Laura smiled, as if she'd just realized

she already knew. "Is it the woman you had me find some new clothes for not too long ago?"

Was he that transparent? "Yeah. Her name's Althea, and you're right. I miss her. I'd planned to go home tonight."

"Home?"

He had started thinking of his place on Big Bear Mountain as home, he guessed, about the time he fell for Althea. "My mountain cabin. The one you keep insisting is in the middle of nowhere," he said, keeping his tone light.

"You can leave after the meeting with the staff in the morning."

"I plan to."

Laura grinned. "In that case, you may want to look over the articles of incorporation Russ sent over, just to make sure everything's the way you want it for your co-op before he files the papers. I have to tell the realtor what name to put on the deed for that land."

Russ Fields, his attorney, had apparently moved even faster than usual. Jared followed Laura to his office, then sat on the leather sofa in the corner. As he read over the papers which established the Big Bear Mountain Craft Cooperative, a charitable organization to which Cain Software would donate start-up capital, he told himself he'd been sweating out Althea's reaction to this for nothing. She couldn't help but be ecstatic when he told her how he was helping make her dream come true.

At least he thought she would. On the way back to the mountains the next day, Jared decided to tell Althea about the land, and his plan to put up a functional facility where women could produce and distribute their mountain crafts.

He got sidetracked, though, as soon as he stepped out of his car.

"Jared."

Althea ran into his arms as soon as he stopped the car as if he'd been gone for weeks, not just three days. She plastered herself against him and kissed him as if she feared tomorrow would never come, and he felt ten feet tall. Invincible. And horny as hell.

He wrapped his arms around her. Her sweet, clean scent filled his nostrils. The tang of her joyful tears tickled his tongue.

"Love me." She rubbed herself against him, apparently not caring that they were outside, at the edge of the clearing, where any unexpected guest would park his car.

His nerve endings crackled, sending urgent signals to his brain. "I will, sweetheart."

She tangled her fingers in his shirt front, then worked at the buttons. "Now." Her fingers scorched his skin as they slid the shirt off his shoulders while her tongue bathed the curve of his neck.

A gentle breeze played on his naked back. It cooled him for a moment. Then the late afternoon sun burned through nature's umbrella of gum and hickory leaves and warmed him again.

Her floral scent surrounded them, mingled with the pungent smell of cedar and the decaying leaves beneath the trees. "Love me now," she said again.

"Here?"

"Oh, yes."

Her need showed in her flushed cheeks, in the wild look in her eyes. He eyed the scratchy-looking pine bark mulch beneath their feet, then considered the tree behind Althea. He backed her against the tree. With one hand, he grasped the front of her skirt while he ripped away the thin cotton panties that barred his way. "Wrap your legs around me." He gripped her buttocks, lifted her, and joined their bodies.

Her tight, wet, heat surrounded him, milked him. She made him want to stay forever. The breeze cooled his bare backside, tickling him like a lover's breath. The pressure built, threatened to explode.

He braced her against the tree trunk, then thrust harder and faster, oblivious to everything but her sweet sex surrounding him. Her fingers dug into his shoulders, her legs clasped him tighter. Her sex convulsed around him, clenched him like a fist as it wrung out his release.

It seemed to last forever, this starburst of sensation, and the spurting, throbbing feeling of completion. He leaned his forehead against the tree's smooth bark and savored each sensation that washed over him.

"Althea?"

She stirred against him. "More?"

He wished. He was getting hard again by the time he lifted her and set her on her feet. Then he stepped back and grinned. "In the house this time?"

"All right." Althea's smile stoked Jared's fire.

Loving him made sex all the sweeter.
Althea sat across from Jared in the hot tub a few

minutes later. She stroked his long, narrow feet and muscular calves made satin-slick by the bath oil that clung to them.

Hot water swirled from the jets behind them. The surface of the tub soon became a froth of foam and bubbles that taunted the sensitized, swollen flesh between her legs. A minty, woodsy scent hung heavy in the hot, damp air, as sensuous as the satiny-slick surface of his skin.

She sank to her knees between his legs and cradled his sex between her hands until it swelled and turned rock hard again. Velvety smooth, silk over steel, it beckoned her lips, her tongue.

As if he knew what she wanted, he stood, a sculpted god obscured in a fragrant fog of man-made steam. She slid her hands down and cupped his heavy sac, then rolled it between her fingers as she leaned forward to catch the tip of his long, thick shaft gently between her teeth.

He shuddered. She snaked out her tongue, stabbed at the tiny slit in the head of his sex, then bathed the length of him with openmouthed kisses and tiny love bites. He tasted salty-sweet, clean. She hadn't thought it possible, but he hardened even more in her hands and mouth. He groaned, as if what she was doing to him made him feel too good. Too much.

Her insides clenched and her nipples tingled. She took one last taste of him. Then she stood and pushed him back on the seat. She sat on his lap, facing him. Feeling his pulsing sex against her own and wanting him more than she'd ever wanted anything before in her life.

"Take me, sweetheart."

He gave her the courage she needed to lift herself up, take him in her hand again to show him the way. She slid down and took him inch by delicious inch; and when she could go no farther, she tightened her inner muscles around him. Being filled with him like this made her want even more.

He seemed to know. He cupped her breasts, then took a straining nipple in his mouth and suckled. He flexed his powerful hips, thrust upward to bury himself in her even deeper. Then he took both her hands, slid them down his body until they tangled in the hair that cushioned their sexes.

"Open up for me."

At first she didn't understand. When his finger tunneled in and found the tiny nub that gave her so much pleasure, she spread her outer lips wide. Now, when he thrust into her, his body stimulated hers, inside and out.

The pressure built. She wanted to sustain it, yet she yearned for release. She rose until she caught the tip of him within her straining flesh, then came down hard. She took all of him. He filled her completely, all the way to her womb. She shuddered at the pleasure-pain and at the incredible feel of his throbbing climax mingling with her own. Spent, she fell against him.

It was some time later when he spoke. "We'd better get out of this tub before we fall asleep."

She tried lifting her head, but found she still couldn't do it. "I can't move."

"Hey, sweetheart, I'm supposed to be the one who's limp as a wet towel about now."

He didn't feel all that limp. As a matter of fact, she got the distinct impression from the way he twitched and thickened inside her that he could be enticed into making love again without a whole lot of trouble.

She couldn't. With effort, she lifted herself off him and climbed out of the hot tub. When he joined her in bed a few minutes later, she gave his half-hard sex an affectionate squeeze. "I missed you," she said sleepily.

"Me, or *that?*"

She laughed, then moved her hand to his beard-roughened cheek. *"That's* part of you. A pretty good-sized part."

"I'm glad you like both of us. By the way, I missed you, too."

"Jared, I—" She couldn't say it. Not while she was still so terribly afraid. But not saying it wouldn't make it any less true. "I love you," she whispered, so quietly she hoped that maybe he wouldn't hear.

He pulled her close, so close his warm breath dampened the sensitive spot of skin where her neck joined her shoulders. "Good. I want you to, sweetheart."

For the first time since they'd become lovers, Althea felt Jared relax completely. For a long time she lay in his arms, listened to his quiet, regular breathing. How long would this idyllic interlude last before something happened? How long would it be before she'd suffer another wrenching loss?

Althea loved him. As he watched her drive slowly down the mountain, Jared wanted to shout the news to the world. But he was anything but certain she wanted the kind of commitment he envisioned between them.

Something about the way she sounded and looked made him think she'd give almost anything not to love him. Grabbing his coffee mug, he went out on the porch, took a spot on the corner of the porch rail. As he listened to the water rush down the mountain, he tried to make sense of the mixed messages Althea kept sending.

That she wanted him was no mystery at all. Her urgency, the hungry way she touched him, even the heated looks she cast at him when she thought he wasn't looking, left no doubt in his mind about her desire.

He wasn't about to question the Fates that had brought her to him without previous lovers to compare with him. That was his good fortune, deserved or not.

But he didn't understand exactly why he roused her passion. It wasn't his money or his success. He was certain he'd recognize the subtle kind of avarice he'd seen in scores of women since he first made a name for himself.

He'd almost say she loved him in spite of his success. Did his wealth intimidate her, make her wary of him?

At the sound of the phone, he tried to dust off his brain. He set his coffee down, unsnapped the portable phone from his belt, and brought it to his ear.

"Cain here."

Laura sounded excited. She'd just gotten a commitment from several businessmen in Blairsville to support the newly formed Big Bear Mountain Craft Cooperative, and Jared's architect had dropped off blueprints for the building.

"Good. The co-op could be operational in less than two months if we can find a contractor to start work on the building right away."

Only one bid had come in so far, and it sounded

high—but it came from Alvin Reese, the general contractor who had built his house. Jared had no doubt the man would do a good job. "I'll talk to him. Maybe he'll lower his price."

After they went over some questions employees had posed yesterday after he left, Jared let Laura go. He dialed a number, intent on tracking down a man about a building. Shortly afterward, he drove down the mountain to meet with Alvin over lunch in Blairsville.

After they came to a verbal agreement about the co-op construction project, Jared strolled across the square to a jewelry store whose sign said it had served the people of Blairsville for more than a hundred fifty years.

He told himself he was only going to look; but when he left the store, he had a small velvet box in his pocket.

TWENTY

As Althea worked quietly on the quilt that night, Jared watched her, imagined them this time next summer. Where would they be?

Here, savoring the peaceful sounds of rushing water, listening to fat squirrels chattering in the trees? Enjoying a peaceful summer evening making love or simply taking pleasure in each other's company?

He smiled. Every minute he could get away from Atlanta, from the demands of his company, they'd be here. This was home. Althea's, and now his again.

Unless . . .

He recalled her brother's ravaged face, the abject terror in his eyes when he didn't know if his wife would live or die. Jared wouldn't risk Althea's life like that. If she were to get pregnant, they'd stay in Atlanta, where the best of care was just around the corner.

She could be pregnant already. Fear gripped Jared, not for himself but for Althea, who'd given him no time last night, no opportunity to protect her. He stared at her flat stomach, imagined it growing round and full with their baby.

The box in his pants pocket jabbed his thigh, a reminder of what he'd decided to do as soon as the ring caught his eye. He got up and crossed the room.

When he reached the quilting frame, he stopped and met her questioning gaze. "Marry me, Althea," he said, as he knelt before her and placed his head in her lap.

Her hands came off the quilt. She dropped her needle. The muscles in her thighs tightened beneath his cheek. "What brought this on?" she asked.

"You love me. I want to spend the rest of my life with you. Seems a proposal's the next logical step."

"For you, maybe. Jared, I'm not sure. Can't we just go along the way we are? See what happens?"

She sounded so frightened, he almost backed off. Then he remembered. "Sweetheart, there may be more than just us to consider. Remember last night?"

At first she looked confused. Then realization apparently dawned. "I remember. But I don't think the timing was right."

He pulled the box from his pocket and flipped it open to reveal the diamond solitaire in its simple platinum setting. "Let's not take a chance."

"Take a chance?" Althea wanted nothing more than to marry Jared, gamble that fate wouldn't wrench him from her arms. But she was so afraid. Afraid he didn't love her. That someday he'd get tired of her and walk away.

"Marry me, sweetheart." As if he knew she couldn't resist his touch, he splayed a hand across her belly as he held her gaze. "Have my babies. Warm my bed. Oh, hell, I don't know how to put it fancy for you, but I want to spend the rest of my life trying to make you happy."

"Where would we live?" She'd dry up in that sterile

condo of his, looking at the four empty walls every day while he escaped to his office.

He took out the ring and slid it onto the finger she'd kept bare since she'd placed Bill's ring in his cold, dry hand before they closed the casket.

"It's a perfect fit," he said, and he brought her hand to his lips.

"I haven't said yes, Jared." She repeated her question about where they'd live, then reminded him she had her own life here—her shop and her teaching job. Her dream for the craft co-op.

He curled his hand around hers, as if to hold her fingers closed around the ring. Then he got up and pulled her over to the couch. "This will be our home, sweetheart."

"What about my work?"

"I'd like for you to do less of it, so you can come with me when I have to spend time in Atlanta. Give up teaching. Hire somebody to work full-time in your shop." As if he feared what she'd say, he tightened his fingers around her hand, held her gaze with sober eyes.

If she gave up her teaching job, she'd never save enough to get the co-op underway—especially if she had to eat away the meager profits of the shop by hiring full-time help. "I can't." But, oh, how she wanted to say yes.

"Why not?" Jared's expression clouded. He reminded her of a plaintive child whose candy she'd taken away last spring before school let out. A child she couldn't help loving. She reached out and touched his cheek.

"The co-op. Jared, I made a promise—"

"Don't worry about your co-op, sweetheart. I'll help you . . ."

"You don't understand. It's something I have to do myself. My dream." Once it had been Bill's dream, too. She couldn't let it die, even though he was gone.

He wiped away the tears she just realized had dampened her cheeks, then pulled her into his arms. "Can't you share your dream with the man you love?"

"You want to help get the co-op off the ground?" She had trouble picturing Jared chasing around the mountains, shaming and cajoling local businessmen into giving the support they'd withdrawn after Bill's death. If he did it, though, she imagined he'd succeed beyond her wildest expectations.

"Sure. I'd give you the moon, if I could find a way to pluck it out of the sky, sweetheart."

She loved him so much. Maybe she—No, she'd fought too hard to relinquish her independence now, to define her life again in terms of someone else's. "I don't need the moon," she said, "and I've got to rely on myself."

"Rely on me, too, sweetheart. I care for you." He paused, then paced, as though he were trying to figure a way around her objections. "Althea, whether you marry me or not, I'm going to help you get that co-op started. If Mom could have had a place like that, we could have stayed here. Your dream's big enough for me to share. Isn't it?"

It was. And if Jared were willing to hit up local merchants for support, who was Althea to stop him? She'd had precious little luck rallying financial backing herself.

"I want you to be my partner." He grinned, as if he realized his battle was finally won.

She knew Jared. No matter how loudly he might protest, he'd take over her life and hand her whatever she wanted. Most of the time, she imagined, he'd give it to her before she figured out that she wanted it. He was that kind of a man.

She could sacrifice a little pride, even give up a bit of the independence she'd fought so hard to achieve. They seemed small enough concessions to make for love.

Then she remembered. As much as he thought he wanted a simple life on the mountain now, he belonged in another world. A world full of movers and shakers, pampered women and powerful men.

"Your life's not only here, Jared. What about Atlanta? Your company? Your friends? Can you honestly tell me I'd fit in?"

Jared raised a questioning eyebrow. "My friends will love you. Anywhere I fit in, so will you." When she didn't respond, he smiled. "I've never been much for the Atlanta social scene, sweetheart. Don't have the pedigree or the inclination."

"Really?"

"Really. I could count on one hand the times, in the past couple of years, that I've had to put on a monkey suit and smile for reporters. Those times would have been easier if I'd had you by my side."

Althea looked down at her finger, at the brilliant light that reflected off facets of the diamond he'd just given her. Maybe their love could last. Maybe the Fates would recall the pain she'd already suffered in this life and look kindly on them now. Whatever the future might hold, she couldn't walk away from Jared, from the dream of love and happily ever after.

"I'll marry you," she told him as she put her arms

around his waist and rested her head against his shoulder. If Althea couldn't find a way to conquer the fear that took the edge off her joy, she'd live with it.

The next day Althea went through the motions at the shop. Every few minutes she glanced at the beautiful ring Jared had put on her finger the night before. Could the love between them last? Could they find joy together?

Before she left this morning, he'd promised her a sensual feast—a promise that had her itching to sample it as she waited on customers . . . and imagining what they'd do in vivid detail every time she had a few moments to herself.

The warm, sunny Saturday in August must have encouraged tourists to come out shopping. Althea sold three full-size quilts and nearly a dozen quilted wall hangings before noon. She'd be able to add a hefty sum to the savings she'd earmarked to buy the land for the co-op, she thought as she took the excess money from the cash register to the back room and hid it in a small drawer.

With Jared's help, she should be able to get the co-op up and running soon. She doubted the men who ran small businesses here in the mountains would balk at pledging their support to him.

Just thinking about him gave her a warm feeling all over. Again, she wondered what delights he had had in mind this morning. She'd find out in less than an hour now, she thought when she checked the time.

"Althea?"

That sounded like Jim. If it were, she hoped he was

in a better mood than he'd been the last time they spoke. "I'm back here," she called out.

He joined her, then set a steaming covered casserole dish onto the work counter. "Mary sent you and Jared a chicken pot pie."

It smelled wonderful. "Tell Mary thanks," she said, as she set it on the table by her purse.

"I asked her to make it. Figured you shouldn't have to cook the night after you two got yourselves engaged."

She glanced at her ring as she tried to recall who had come into the shop today that might have run into her brother afterward. "How did you know?"

"Cain drove by the house this morning. He's a good man, and he'll take care of you. What do you say we bury the hatchet and forget about that little argument we had last week?"

Jim hardly ever strung that many words together. He must have been practicing his speech, all the way here from his place on Cherokee Ridge. "So, Jared's all right now, since he gave me a ring?"

"Come on, little sister, I'm just trying to look out for you, the way I promised our folks I'd do."

"Well, is it all right?"

Jim frowned, then changed the subject. "When's the wedding? Jared said I had to ask you."

"I just agreed to get engaged last night. We haven't discussed when we . . ." Oh, no. Althea took a deep breath to calm her racing pulse. The significance of what she'd done finally registered in her brain. She hadn't just agreed to get engaged. She'd agreed to marry Jared Cain. "Not too soon, I don't guess."

"I got the feeling tomorrow would suit Jared fine."

She figured an immediate wedding would probably thrill Jim, too. "It wouldn't suit me. I've got to do a million things before I can even think about getting married. Come on, let's step out front, in case a customer comes in."

"Things to do? Like what?" Jim's thoughtful frown grew into a full-blown scowl when he leaned against the counter in front of the cash register.

"Like quitting my teaching job and finding somebody to work full-time in the store so I can get the co-op started. Jared said he'd help get businessmen around here to back it." Suddenly she remembered Jared's quilt and her purely selfish desire to see him wrapped up in it like a Christmas package. "I've got to finish his quilt, too."

"Lame excuses. You could do all those things just as well married as single."

That was what Jared had said last night, only he'd put it in prettier terms. Maybe they both were right. She felt as though she'd stepped on a moving train when she took Jared's ring, a train that wasn't about to stop until she stood with him in front of a preacher and became his wife.

She'd worked so hard to stand on her own two feet, not depend on others to do what she needed done. "Jim, we'll get married soon enough," she said, hoping that would get him out of her hair for a little while.

"Mary said she'd fix the cake, get the ladies at the church to make sandwiches and such."

Althea made herself smile. "Tell Mary thanks." A country reception in the churchyard under the big oak tree, in plain sight of the graveyard with its colorful plastic flower arrangements didn't appeal. It wouldn't have, even if she were planning to marry a boy who'd never left the northeast Georgia mountains. It would be too much like the wedding celebration she'd had to cancel.

"That okay? I mean, Bill and all—"

She wanted to hug her brother. He understood more than he let on. "No. It isn't. But it's not just Bill. I'd rather we did it quietly." Her way. Not Jim and Mary's. And not Jared's, either. "I've already told Jared I don't want any big, fancy ceremony."

"All right. Just let me know when it's going to be, and we'll be there. Cain will be good for you." With that, Jim turned and strode away, leaving her at the door to stare at his back until he climbed into his van.

For the next hour, she straightened stock, stopping every now and then to wait on a customer. As Althea headed up Big Bear Mountain, Mary's pot pie still warm on the seat beside her, she let herself imagine what Jared had in store for them tonight.

He was the luckiest man alive. Jared leaned back in the rocker on the porch and listened to a squawking crow in the distance. His gaze wandered toward the winding road, then settled on a flowering bush tucked in the bend. Althea would know the name of those flowers. Whatever they were, they reminded him of her, all pink and white and delicate. His nostrils flared as he imagined them exuding her sweet, light scent.

A car engine labored. Tires crunched along the gravel road. Jared checked his watch, then got up and moved to the porch rail. As soon as Althea's Pathfinder stopped, he hurried to open her door.

"Welcome home," he told her.

TWENTY-ONE

"I missed you." Althea leaned over the pot pie in her hands, brushed a kiss across Jared's jaw. "Mary sent our supper."

"I thought we'd go out."

She smiled as she stepped inside the house. "I'd rather stay here. Work on your quilt or—"

"Play?"

The promise in her eyes sent sparks flying below his belt. She made him feel like the sexiest guy on the planet, and he loved it.

"That, too," she told him.

He took the hot dish to the kitchen and set it in the oven. "Hungry?"

She looked him over head to toe, then moved closer, so close her breath tickled his chest through his shirt. "Are you?"

"Yeah. For you, sweetheart. But we'd better eat first. Keep our strength up."

"Okay." Smiling, she took out plates and silverware and set the table. "You're a nice man, Jared Cain. Not every man would have taken the trouble to go see Jim, especially after the ruckus he raised about our—"

"He had the right to be upset. I would have been,

if it had been my sister carrying on with some city slicker the way you've been carrying on with me." Jared dodged the potholder Althea tossed at him.

"It's not funny. Come on, let's eat."

Jared made a mental note to tease Althea more often. She was cute when she pouted. After she sat down, he joined her and dug into the casserole dish. "What is this?" he asked, suspicious of any meal whose main ingredients he couldn't readily identify.

Althea took a bite, chewed slowly, then swallowed. "Chicken something-or-other, I think."

"You'd better not even consider serving me something-or-other anything." He was only half joking.

"Or what?"

"Or I just might have to show you who's the boss." Jared grinned, fished out something he thought looked like a piece of celery. He couldn't stand celery unless it was raw.

"Oh, yeah?"

"Yeah."

Althea grinned. "Well, we aren't married yet, and if you don't want me to think twice about taking that step, you'd better stop sounding like a tyrant."

Jared's mind wandered to that night not too long ago before he'd left for Atlanta. "I thought you enjoyed letting me show you I'm the boss."

"Well—" Her blush gave her away as certainly as if she'd come right out and told him she remembered. "Yes. When you show me *that* way, I kind of like being under your spell."

"Under me, you said?"

"That, too."

Jared ate his dinner, but he had no idea whether it

tasted good or bad or whether the main ingredient had been fish or fowl. He was so hard, he ached. Being in lust was heaven and hell.

He couldn't wait for Althea to swallow her last bite of food. "You're finished with that."

"I am?"

"Yes. Let's go upstairs." He scooped her up in his arms.

She laughed. "Jared, what's the hurry?"

"I'm horny."

"Well, you're the one who said you wanted to eat first."

"Now I want dessert." He squeezed her tighter against his chest as he took the stairs, two at the time. When he got to the shower doors, he slid her down his body, then peeled off their clothes.

"Go on, get in the shower and turn the water on."

When he stepped in behind her, he was hit by an icy stream. "That ought to cool you off some," she told him with a sassy grin.

"Don't count on it, sweetheart." Her lascivious glance down his torso more than made up for the water's chilling effects. "Water's getting warm now."

A heady fragrance of herbs and spices soon filled the air when he smoothed scented soap over her satin-smooth skin.

Her nipples tightened at his touch. Her beautiful breasts filled his hands. "You like this as much as I do."

When she looked at him, fire in her gaze, he nearly lost it. "Yeah. I like it a lot," she said, her tone ragged.

He went down on his knees and rubbed his cheek against the soft hair between her legs. Gently, he spread her outer lips, caressed her with the pad of his thumb as he waited with his mouth.

He throbbed. As he lapped her with his tongue and nibbled her tiny jewel with his teeth, his pulse raced. He took her in his mouth and suckled her the way she had him. With one finger, then two, he delved inside. She was ready, and so was he.

She shuddered, moaned, then leaned back against the shower wall. Hot water sluiced down her body, over his head. When he felt her muscles slacken, he stood and gathered her in his arms. Reaching over her shoulder, he turned off the shower.

"Let's try this on a bed." He wrapped her in a towel, then rubbed one over his own aching flesh.

When she reached for him after they had crawled into bed, he thought he'd explode.

"Better do that later."

"No." As if she she sensed how close he was to the edge, she sheathed him, straddled him, and guided him home. Her rhythm started out first slow and gentle, but quickly built to a fever pitch.

He wanted her to come with him, but he was close. Too close. "Slow down, sweetheart. I can't—"

"Don't wait. Let go."

He did, and when he came, she followed. For a long time they lay there, spent. Content. Jared looked forward to years more of times like this in Althea's arms.

He looked forward even more to making love to her again, as soon as he could catch his breath.

Althea was glad she didn't open her shop on Sunday or Monday. The time she'd spent alone with Jared had been a dream come true. And she still had today to look forward to, after she took care of a few errands in town. Smiling, she slipped on her clothes and went downstairs.

"Good morning, sweetheart." His voice, deep and sexy, sent tingles down her spine. "Where are you headed off to?"

She poured a cup of coffee and stirred sugar into it before joining him at the table. "Blairsville. I need to let the school board know I won't be teaching this fall."

"Wouldn't a letter do?"

"I wrote one, but I want to deliver it in person. It's awfully late for me to be canceling my contract."

He smiled. "Want me to go with you?"

"There's no need. The superintendent of schools will understand."

"Are you ready to set a date?"

She loved the way the faint laugh lines around his mouth and eyes showed when he grinned. "Not yet. I want to get the co-op started first."

Jared took her hand. "It will be. Trust me."

"Have you talked to any businessmen yet?"

"Laura has."

Had he been having his assistant talk to folks about the co-op from their office in Atlanta? "I thought you were going to do this yourself . . ."

"I am. Laura's been doing some legwork for me, that's all." He gave her hand a squeeze, as if to reassure her.

Althea glanced at the ring on her finger occasionally as she sipped her coffee. "When do you think you'll have the backing we need? I want to buy the land and get the building fixed up enough so women can work on their crafts there this winter."

"Soon." Jared shot her an enigmatic smile that stayed in the back of her mind as she drove to Blairsville and went about her errands.

It seemed everybody in town knew about her and Jared even before they spotted the ring on her finger. Feeling indulgent about being the main topic of gossip for the moment, Althea accepted good-natured wishes for their happiness as she made her way to the school board office in the courthouse.

"Morning, Lucy." As she stepped inside, she greeted the secretary who'd been working for the county school system ever since she could remember.

Lucy's grin could have lit up the town square. "Figured I'd be seein' you, girl. Give me your hand. Let me see that big diamond ring Lenny over at the jeweler's has been bragging that he sold to your city slicker the other day."

"This one?" She held out her left hand and braced herself for more of the oohs and ahs she'd already heard from people who'd caught her while she was walking here from her parking place on the east side of the square.

"My, my. You've gone and caught yourself a live one. Congratulations. You deserve to be happy." The older woman's smile faded, then came back brighter than ever. "When's the big day?"

"We haven't decided. I have made up my mind not to teach this year, though; so, I thought I'd better let you know now so you can find somebody to take my place." Althea handed over a sealed envelope. "Here. This should make my resignation official enough to satisfy the board."

"Never thought I'd see the day I'd be glad you quit, girl, but I am. Now we've got a spot for Dora Littleton."

"Dora's back in town?"

Lucy frowned. "Got here last week. She finally found the backbone to get rid of that louse she married. Pity she didn't do it before she had those two precious little boys."

"I didn't know." The last Althea had heard, Dora was still living in Chattanooga. She'd given up her teaching job two years ago to follow him there. "I feel bad for her."

"Well, she's hard up. Got nothing when she divorced him. The woman never had a lick of common sense, but she's a good teacher. Hard to figure."

It was. Althea felt good, knowing her last minute resignation had opened the door for Dora.

After she chatted a few minutes with Lucy, Althea stopped by the bank. The sale of that big quilt yesterday had fattened the deposit she needed to make; and if she figured correctly, she'd have close to six thousand dollars in her nest egg—only two thousand short of the down payment she needed to buy that piece of land Harriet Tucker had been trying to sell her for two years now. Maybe the bank would loan her more, now that Jared—or rather his assistant—had persuaded some local businessmen to pledge their support.

"Althea. Let me see your ring."

"When's the wedding going to be?"

Was there nothing else happening that folks deemed

worthy of idle gossiping over? Shaking her head, Althea joined two former classmates who were having iced tea at one of the tables on the sidewalk outside Yoder's Restaurant. "Good morning to you, too," she said with a shake of her head.

Mona Runnels grabbed her hand. "Wow. How much did that rock cost?"

"Mona, you've got the manners of an ape. Althea, don't pay her any mind." Betty Lane, Mona's sister, snatched Althea's hand away, then made a big show out of inspecting the ring. "I don't think I've ever seen a diamond quite that big," she said when she finally released Althea's hand.

"So, tell us, when's the wedding going to be? Are you going to do it fancy, like the ones they show on daytime TV?" Mona's gaze kept returning to Althea's finger, as if she were thinking envious—if not larcenous—thoughts.

"We haven't decided yet."

"Why not?" Betty asked. "I tell you, girl, if I had that man on the hook, I'd hustle him in front of the preacher before he could bat an eye."

Mona made a snorting sound. "And you think I've got no manners, when you go drooling over Althea's intended like he was a piece of prime beef behind the butcher's counter. He is fine, though. Can't deny that."

Althea laughed. "I'm partial to him."

They chatted for a while, until Althea saw an opportunity to get away. "This is the only day I'm off this week. There must be a million things I have to do," she said after declining a refill of iced tea. "It was good to see you two."

Everybody knew, and everybody was talking about

her and Jared; but it seemed they all wished her well, so Althea couldn't complain too much that they apparently had no concept of minding their own business. On an impulse, she decided to stop by Harriet Tucker's office before heading home.

"Althea. What a surprise!"

"Hello, Harriet."

The older woman smiled, her perfectly made-up face crackling a bit with the motion. "I hear congratulations are in order."

Althea felt a bit out of place in her simple skirt and top when she took in the realtor's crisply tailored navy suit and white silk blouse. "Yes. Thank you."

"Your young man's quite a catch."

How would Harriet know Jared? Then Althea remembered. She had been the realtor who'd sold Big Bear Mountain to him. The woman's commission on that deal had to have been enough to ensure Jared a cozy spot in her memory for a long time to come.

"I think he's pretty wonderful," she said for what seemed like the twentieth time since she'd gotten to town. Frankly she was getting tired of hearing folks imply Jared's most appealing quality was the size of his bank balance, because there was so much more to him than that. So much to love that had nothing to do with his business acumen or his wealth.

"Do you still have that piece of property I've been wanting for the craft co-op?" Althea asked, hoping to put the subject of her good fortune to rest.

Harriet looked perplexed. "Why, yes, I do. But why would you want it now?"

"Why wouldn't I?" Now Althea was confused.

"Because—oh, my, I don't know if I'm supposed to be telling you . . ."

"Telling me what?"

Harriet picked up a pair of designer glasses from the desk and set them on her nose. She met Althea's gaze. "The land for the co-op's already been bought. I closed the deal on it last week."

"Why . . . you said it was still available."

"That piece of property you've been looking at is still for sale. Probably will be ten years down the road, for that matter."

Harriet didn't need to remind Althea that the property wasn't prime. She knew that. Its negative features were what made it cheap. "What did you mean, then, when you said someone bought the land for the co-op?"

"What I said. Your young man picked out another site, one where trucks can get in and out." She described the property, which Althea recognized as being at a crossroads a mile or two down the highway from her shop, across from an old rock quarry. "He hired Alvin Reese to put up a building. They should be grading the site today, from what I heard."

No. Harriet had to be mistaken. Jared wouldn't . . . would he? "Are you sure he's not building a new factory on that land?"

"Honey, no. Jared made it real clear from the first time we talked that he wanted to build a co-op for you—and for his sweet mama's memory. He mentioned how hard it's been for you to get donations to get it started. You ought to be thrilled."

Thrilled? Althea's temples throbbed, and her vision blurred. "How? There's all kinds of paperwork—"

"He no more than said he wanted the land than his

assistant down in Atlanta—Laura's her name—got his lawyer to draw up the papers for the co-op, file the tax exemption application, and so on. By the time Laura wore the seller down on the price, everything was all in order. Jared Cain doesn't leave anything to chance." Harriet sounded as though she thought Jared could do no wrong.

Althea didn't agree. She felt tears well up in her eyes, but she refused to shed them in front of the realtor. "I've got to go," she said, as she got up and bolted for the door. When she got to her car, she laid her head against the steering wheel and cried.

Where was Althea? Jared walked over to the quilt stand. Bored without her here, he tried to guess how many tiny stitches she'd placed in the quilt that had brought her to him in the first place. Millions, he imagined. The quilt was almost finished.

He glanced at his watch and wondered how much longer her errands would take. Alvin had called from the co-op site and said his men had taken out the old concrete slab. They were about to start grading the area where the building would go.

It was three o'clock now. He could drive over and make certain that Alvin had staked out the right spot for the building. Or he could wait and take a look tomorrow while Althea was working.

Jared opted to go now. After all, Althea might be shopping for hours if she was like most women. He grabbed his keys.

As he drove down to the highway, he tried to decide when he'd tell her. Now that he knew she was willing to let him help her, the timing didn't matter all that much. He felt great when he imagined how happy she'd be to see the site he'd found.

Maybe he'd tell her right away. No, he decided. He'd wait until Alvin had the building's foundation in place, so she could visualize her co-op and realize it would be ready for business very soon.

Five minutes later, he reached the crossroads. Alvin hadn't wasted any time. He'd set his dusty construction trailer up on a corner of what would be the parking lot, next to a grader and what looked like a small bulldozer. The rotund contractor himself stood beside the trailer with a set of blueprints, talking with two workers.

Jared got out of his car and headed for the trailer. When he heard a woman call his name, he stopped in midstride.

Althea. Someone had told her. Whoever it was had spoiled the surprise he'd planned to spring on her next week.

He turned and smiled at her from across the clearing. It wasn't until he saw the tear stains on her face that Jared realized something was wrong. Bad wrong.

TWENTY-TWO

"Jared, how could you?"

"How could I what, sweetheart?"

Althea waved her hand at the raw earth, then at the flags that marked where the corners of the building would be. "How could you go behind my back? Do this. Do what I wanted to do for myself."

"You said you'd let me help," he said, his defenses suddenly on alert.

"You call this helping? I call it taking over. What possessed you to think you'd please me by bulldozing in, showing me up?" She looked mad enough to commit murder.

So much for her having told him she'd accept his help. "Althea, be reasonable. If something's worth doing, it's worth doing right. Your co-op will get a decent start. It owns this land and the building that's going up on it next week, free and clear. We can get local businesses to help with start-up costs once we've got a place . . ."

"Darn it, Jared. Why didn't you ask me before you did this?"

"I wanted to surprise you."

"Surprise? Try shock."

"Would you believe an engagement present?" He watched her fingernails dig into her palms, imagined them digging into his hide.

"No, Jared. Do you always charge in like a bull in a china shop, throw your money around to buy whatever it is you think you want?"

"No. Sweetheart, be reasonable. You wanted donations from businesses. That's all this is. A donation from Cain Software. It's likely that the donation will save the company as much in taxes as it will cost."

"I don't believe you. I don't believe this."

Althea whirled around and stomped off toward her car. Red dust swirled in the breeze, leaving Jared coated with it by the time she sped away.

Alvin ambled over, an amused look on his florid face. "Independent little cuss, ain't she?" he said.

"That she is," Jared replied.

"Want to scrap this project?"

"No way. But I'd better go after her and see if I can talk my way back into her good graces." A feeling of dread rose in Jared's throat. He'd never been much good at sweet-talking angry women.

"I've never been so mad in my entire life. How could he?" Althea pulled up in front of the churchyard under a big hickory tree, then got out of the car. A brisk breeze fanned her cheeks but did little to cool her anger.

Did she come across to everyone as a wimp? Why did no one who cared for her seem to think she could do the smallest thing on her own? She went straight to the simple stones that marked her parents' graves.

Needing some task to take her mind off Jared and his perfidy, she straightened the plastic flowers in a marble vase between the two markers.

It had begun with them, this . . . this insistence on doing for her, not giving her a chance to achieve anything on her own. Althea had no quarrel with her mom or dad, for she'd been their child. She'd needed their protection and guidance.

Their legacy, though, had passed on to Jim, who hadn't stepped back, let her grow up and make her own mistakes. He, in turn, had turned her over to Bill.

Bill. Something drew her to his grave. Had he given her free rein and let her make her own decisions? Or had it just happened that his wants had paralleled hers?

She had a feeling her needs and Bill's had been well-attuned to one another—but she'd never know now. She had certainly leaned on Bill. She'd counted on his help to get local businesses to support the co-op. When he died, she'd vowed to do it on her own.

Jared had used his money to buy what she'd wanted to earn. As much as she loved him, Althea didn't believe she could forgive him.

Before she felt Jared's hands on her shoulders, she sensed his presence. In spite of everything, he made her go warm and wet inside, but she fought back the desire she didn't want, wouldn't accept, but couldn't squelch.

"Why are you here?" she asked, refusing to turn and face him.

"Because you are. Althea, I wanted to please you, not make you angry."

"I promised myself I'd get a co-op going. That *I'd* do it. Me, Jared. Not you."

He squeezed her shoulders, then moved to her side and knelt. For a long time, he stared at the inscription on the creamy marble slab. When he stood back up, he looked her in the eye. "For him?" he asked.

"For myself." Even as she said it, she wondered if it were true. The co-op had been Bill's dream first, a dream he'd dreamed too late to save his sister from her vicious husband or the granny who'd raised him from dying in gut-wrenching poverty. He'd hoped the co-op would save other women from similar fates. Had Althea merely gone along, made her dead fiancé's dream her own?

"Why don't you want me to help, then? You say you love me."

"Help? I don't call what you've done help. You've barged right in, taken over."

He took her hand. "All I did was find a piece of land and hire someone to put up a building on it."

It sounded like no big deal when he said it, until Althea thought of how much money he must have spent. Until she remembered the little piece of property she'd struggled to save enough to put a down payment on and her plan to make do with the rickety old building that had been there as long as she remembered.

"That's all?" She couldn't help the sarcastic tone that edged into her voice.

Jared apparently thought she was being serious. "That's all, sweetheart. Except for having Laura make some calls to extract promises for operating capital donations from businesses in Blairsville and Dahlonega. What gets done inside that building will be strictly up to you."

He sounded so earnest, she couldn't stay angry. She

met his gaze and tried to smile. "I can understand your wanting to surprise me. But what you've done is too much. You didn't ask me or even tell me ahead of time what you were doing. You must have had some idea how important it is to me to do things on my own."

"I did. And knowing that gave me a few uncomfortable moments—until you told me you'd let me help."

His little-boy grin made her want to hug him, even as it fueled her uncertainty about their future. "Your idea of helping is taking over. Jared, I can't let you run my life. I don't know if I can marry you, but I know I can't live in your pocket the way I've been doing. I need time to myself. Time to think."

She met his gaze, sensed his confusion and hurt. Well, she was hurting, too. And he was the reason why. "I'll follow you to your place and gather my things. We need some time apart."

"What about the quilt?"

Althea pictured it on its stand beside the fireplace. "It's nearly finished. I could—"

"Stay. Finish it where it is, sweetheart. I'll clear out. I'll spend a week or so in Atlanta so you can have your space."

He sounded so reasonable. So accommodating. She wished she didn't have to give him back his ring. It hurt when she pressed it gently into his hand. No matter what, she loved Jared. Wanted him.

But she couldn't let him control her life and destroy the sense of independence she'd worked so hard to obtain. "Jared, keep this. I can't wear it now," she said, her voice cracking with the effort to hold back tears.

For a minute, she thought he would protest, but he slipped the ring into his shirt pocket. "For what it's worth, I'm sorry you think I did something I shouldn't have, but I knew how much it would mean to you to have the co-op up and running. I didn't think it would matter so much how that came about."

"It does."

"I know now. If I could, I'd go back in time. Tell you what I was planning before I went ahead and did it."

"You would?"

"Yeah. If I had, though, and you'd have told me not to do it, a lot of women in these mountains might have had to wait a lot longer than they're going to now to get the same kind of independence that means so much to you."

What he said made sense. Still, she wasn't ready to concede that what he'd done was right. "Might, Jared. I've saved almost enough for the down payment on the place I told you about—not the palace I imagine you're having Alvin build, I'm sure, but one poor mountain women would have been just as happy about having."

He reached over and caressed her jaw. As angry as she was, she couldn't help wishing he'd take her in his arms and love her.

"They'll be more comfortable than they would have been in that rickety shack you wanted to buy," he said, his tone mild.

She couldn't refute that. Still, he'd taken over. He'd made decisions that should have been hers. Made her lose him as surely as if one of them had died. She turned away and stared across the cemetery at her parents' graves.

No matter how much she loved him, she couldn't

give in on this. She couldn't hand over control of her life to this man.

"Give me half an hour to throw a few things in the car, and I'll be gone." He sounded unbelievably sad. "How long will it take you to finish the quilt?" he asked a moment later.

Without Jared and the delicious distraction of making love with him? "It shouldn't take long at all. I should be able to finish it this week."

"Then I'll be back on Sunday. Think about me, sweetheart. Think about us. I haven't changed my mind about what I want." With that, he strode away.

The powerful engine of his Mercedes roared, then faded away in the distance. Jared had really left her. Althea stood in the cemetery staring at cold marble stones. Despite the warm summer sunshine, she shivered. Alone was a lonely place to be.

He hadn't felt so deserted since the day his mom died. Marcie's defection hadn't left Jared fighting nausea, feeling as though he stood alone against the world, without a friend. Like the robot Marcie had once said he was, he opened the door to his Atlanta condo a little after midnight and stepped inside.

But he wasn't a robot. Not with Althea. He recalled that late-night encounter in the shower before he'd come back to Atlanta the last time. The way Althea had initiated and he'd taken over and finished the most exhilarating sexual experience of his life.

The wrung-out, boneless woman he'd carried back to bed had epitomized satisfaction. The satisfied smile on her face and the way she'd snuggled up to him and nibbled at his neck had revealed more clearly than words that she'd just come back from paradise—a paradise he'd given her.

Good sex, he figured, stemmed from getting the right two people together . . . and he and Althea had to be a match made in heaven, if his theory held water.

The last thing he'd wanted was to leave her. Several times on the way here he'd stopped and almost turned around, before reminding himself he'd promised her time away from him. Damn it, he wouldn't let her toss away what they'd found together over something as trivial as his buying her a little gift.

Okay, so the land and building for the co-op were more than a little present, at least in her eyes. He popped the cap off a beer, then sank onto the sofa and stared out at the Atlanta skyline.

He had to figure out what to do to get her back.

By morning he'd downed the better part of a twelve-pack. But he'd managed to come up with a plan.

And developed one hell of a headache, he thought as he dialed Laura at home. He'd get this done, then spend the day trying to catch up on sleep. "Laura?" he said when she picked up the phone.

The receiver suddenly felt heavy, so he switched on the speaker and set the handset down. "Jared, it's barely six o'clock," From her grumpy response, he guessed Laura wasn't happy to hear his voice. Too bad.

"Sorry. I've got a job for you. I want you to pick me out five presents."

"Presents?" Laura asked.

"For Althea. She's mad at me."

"She's not the only one. What do you have in mind?"

Jared thought about that, but came up empty-handed. "Don't know. Something pretty. Sparkly. Expensive. Show her—"

"Jared, are you drunk?"

"Nah. Well, maybe a little. That's it. Jewelry. Get her some jewelry. Ice blue. Like her eyes. Fiery hot." He paused to down the last of the beer. "Nasty stuff. I hate warm beer."

"Aquamarines and rubies?"

Laura's sarcasm went almost but not quite over Jared's aching head. "Not in the same jewelry. You know what I mean. I want to send her one piece every day this week, so she won't forget me while I'm gone. Take care of it."

"Okay. I take it you're here in Atlanta?" Laura sounded as if she were finally waking up.

"Yeah. I'll come to the office tomorrow." Jared mumbled out instructions as to where to have Althea's gifts delivered, then hung up. He kicked off his shoes and lay back against the leather cushions on the sofa.

TWENTY-THREE

By four o'clock on Tuesday, Althea was ready to drop. Thank heaven she hadn't had a lot of customers. She rubbed her gritty eyes. Her shoulders and back ached, and the fingers on her right hand felt as though they were still clutching a quilting needle.

She'd never recommend that her worst enemy pass a sleepless night by quilting for twelve hours straight, the way she'd done last night. Closing early wouldn't hurt anything just this once, she decided. Even the simple task of emptying the cash register seemed too much to ask of her exhausted muscles today.

Gravel crunched outside. Just her luck. Althea slammed the cash drawer shut and tried to paste on a semblance of a smile.

It was Trina. Althea wished she hadn't asked her to drop by when she saw her in town yesterday morning. Now wasn't the time to arrange for her friend to work full-time, not when she wasn't at all certain she'd need the help.

Trina set down her quilted tote bag. "Where's your ring?" she asked.

It would have been too much for Althea to expect

Trina or anyone else not to notice she wasn't wearing the showy ring. "I'm reconsidering Jared's proposal."

"What happened?"

Althea told Trina about Jared's buying the land for the co-op and arranging for a building to be put up. "He barged right in and took over. I won't let anybody, ever again, make me dependent on them." She rubbed her aching temples as she wished again that she hadn't asked Trina to drop by.

"Girl, you've been fretting for months because you couldn't get businesses to donate enough money so you could get a place to start this co-op thing. Now your man's taken care of that problem for you. The way I see it, looking a gift horse in the mouth just don't make sense."

Trina paused as a truck labored up the mountainside, its gears grinding when the driver downshifted to make the steep grade. When Althea glanced toward the highway, she shook her head. Another one of Alvin's dump trucks, full of landfill from Jared's folly at the crossroads just down the hill.

"You hear me, girl?"

"Yes, Trina. But he should have talked to me about it. He shouldn't have just taken over. We're not talking about a few dollars here. Jared's spent a fortune."

"For you, maybe. Think. The man bought himself a mountain. Not an acre or two for a summer place, the way most rich tourists do, but an entire mountain. Setting you up with a place for your co-op's no big deal for a man like him."

Suddenly it hit Althea. Her problem with Jared wasn't exactly that he'd undermined her independence. It wasn't even that he had an annoying tendency to get her whatever he thought she wanted before she voiced a request.

Her problem was that she knew Jared was out of her league, and that she was in over her head. Way over her head. She had no idea how to fight her way to the surface. She'd thought about it more than once before shoving that particular worry to the back of her mind.

"Althea? You all right?" Trina asked.

Too stunned to speak, she shook her head.

"You don't look all right. You look downright peaked."

Althea didn't doubt that. Her cheeks felt cold, as if all the warmth had drained out of her body. "I've got to go outside, get warm."

The sunlight didn't warm her the way it should have when she stepped onto the porch. Instead, she shivered more as she watched a convoy of Alvin's dump trucks lumbering up the mountain highway.

What have I done? Althea asked herself as Trina drove away. Drained, she went inside and gathered her things so she could leave.

"Miss Simmons?"

Althea blinked, then forced her tired eyes to focus. She hadn't heard him drive up, but she had more company. A man in a black suit, cap in hand, stood in the doorway of the shop. He'd apparently arrived in the somber-looking limousine parked outside. "Yes?" she asked, confused.

"I've been asked to bring you this," he said, holding out a small, flat box wrapped in silver foil. "If you'll just sign the receipt—"

"Where did you come from?"

"Atlanta, ma'am."

"From Jared Cain?" What had Jared gone and done now?

"From B. Delavan, Fine Jewelers, ma'am. If you'll sign this, I'll be on my way. It's a long drive back, and I'm not too keen on driving in the mountains at night."

Althea scribbled her name. As the man placed the package in her hand, she eyed it with suspicion. It was heavier than it looked, and plain but for an embossed silver seal on one corner. "Thank you," she murmured, mindful of the manners her mom had taught her.

An hour later she sat at the kitchen table at Jared's place, her gaze fixed on the unopened package. From moment to moment, she vacillated between wanting to see what it contained and fearing she'd find yet another piece of evidence that falling in love with Jared was the worst mistake she'd ever made.

The beer had been a mistake. A bad one. Hammers pounded in Jared's head, as if to remind him he'd exceeded his usual limit of two last night by more than he cared to think about. He blinked at his disheveled image in the bathroom mirror, then splashed cold water into his bleary eyes.

After a long warm shower, he felt better. Vaguely, he remembered his early morning call to Laura. What had he done?

Suddenly Jared knew without a doubt that Althea would not appreciate the costly jewelry he thought he recalled telling Laura to send her. Hell, getting fancy baubles would do nothing but remind her how mad she was at him about buying the land and contracting with Alvin to build the co-op.

So much for his brain on beer. He glanced at his watch as he slid it onto his wrist. Seven o'clock. P.M., not A.M. If Laura had been her usual efficient self, Althea would have the first of his ill-conceived gifts by now.

He sat on the bed and picked up the phone. He even punched out the number at his cabin, but before the call had time to go through, he hung up. He'd promised Althea a week—and he wouldn't go back on his word.

Instead, he called Laura. When she confirmed that she'd carried out his instructions, he silently cursed the woman's efficiency.

Althea got an aquamarine-and-diamond pendant today. Matching earrings would arrive tomorrow. Then a dinner ring and a tennis bracelet. A five-carat ruby carved in the shape of a heart and dangling from a gold chain would arrive on Saturday, the day before he'd told her he'd be back.

Fire and ice. Like her. However angry the gifts might make her, he wanted her to have them.

Maybe she'd would think they were fake. Fat chance. She'd seen his place on Big Bear Mountain and his 550SL coupe. It had to be obvious to her, to anybody with a brain who knew him, that Jared Cain chose quality and damn the cost. She'd hardly believe he'd started cutting corners when he was trying to impress the woman he loved.

"I love her."

When he looked around the empty room, he realized he'd spoken aloud. He repeated the words. They rolled easily off his tongue. Too easily. But panic didn't rise up in his gut the way he expected. Instead, the realization gave him a sort of inner peace. "I love Althea."

He wandered into the living room and gathered up empty longneck bottles, then tossed them in the recycling bin under the bar.

As if Althea were here with him, he sensed her presence. What was she doing? Did she miss him? He imagined she'd be quilting now, drawing her needle in and out of muted green and navy blue prints, following the edges of each small rectangle that made up larger squares. He closed his eyes and imagined her long, slender fingers, pale against the darkness of the quilt's forest green border.

Gentle. Her hands were so calming, so restful, on the quilt or on her little niece's soft, plump body. On his cheek the night she'd told him she loved him.

He'd needed Marcie to be his business partner, stand beside him in a world where he often felt alienated. Watching her walk away had left him vaguely disappointed.

Losing Althea would decimate him. He needed her to make him whole. To fill a void in his heart that he'd never realized was there until now.

She was his other half. His better half. The half he'd begun to miss without realizing it, before he'd decided to go home and seek the elusive something he'd sensed had been missing from his life.

He felt Althea's presence everywhere. In the kitchen where she'd fixed them lunch and in the bedroom where she'd slept away the morning after they learned her sister-in-law was out of danger. Althea was his heart. His home.

If he had to, he'd get down on his knees and spill out the words of love he'd never been able to say before. Maybe they wouldn't come so hard now, since his feelings had suddenly become crystal clear.

Hard or easy, Jared would do whatever it took to keep from losing the only woman who had ever given him unconditional love. He'd even give her the four more days she'd asked for, with only the gifts he was certain would make her more angry than thrilled, to remind her he wanted to be the half that made her whole.

Jared's bed felt terribly big, empty, without him sharing it. Althea rolled over, hugging a pillow that made a poor excuse for his warm, muscular body. She should have gone back to her own cabin tonight, right after she'd put the final stitch into Jared's quilt.

Funny, she felt his presence less in this room, where they'd made love and slept in each other's arms, than downstairs. Or outside, on the mountain he'd come back to, apparently searching for something that was missing from his privileged life.

The geese would fly away from the mountains, but someday they'd come back. Like a wanderer who has finally come home.

Jared had said something like that the day they met, she recalled. Maybe he did belong here, more than in his costly, sterile condo in Atlanta. With her.

Maybe he really was a wanderer who had come home.

She rolled over, burying her face in a pillow that smelled faintly of his cologne. Oh, how she wanted to believe his world and hers weren't so far apart that they could never meet.

Moonlight shone through the wall of windows. Its soft light reflected off small diamonds that surrounded bigger pale blue stones in all but the latest of Jared's gifts. Why had she left them on the nightstand, where she couldn't miss seeing them sparkle in the light of the full moon? Silently they mocked her hopeful conjecture as they confirmed what she knew deep inside.

Jared might have been born in a cabin at the top of Big Bear Mountain, but his world now was miles from here. Miles from her own small universe.

She didn't belong in a world where men bought mountains to indulge nostalgia and gave costly treasures as though they were dime-store trinkets. Jared might call himself a simple man. He might even believe he yearned for simple pleasures. But saying and being weren't the same.

Sleep wouldn't come. She rolled over once again, then got up and sat on the edge of Jared's big oak bed. She stared at the present that had arrived this afternoon. It was different from the rest—a bloodred, heart-shaped ruby on a thin gold chain.

Why had he chosen presents that underscored the chasm between them? Why couldn't he have sent her a simple bouquet of native flowers or made a quick call to say he loved her, the way Bill would have done?

TWENTY-FOUR

"What would you do?"

The sound of his own voice made Jared take a step back. The full moon shone on flat markers and towering monuments in the little graveyard, lending an eerie quality to the night. He shuddered at the plaintive howl of a lone wolf in the distance as he knelt beside the marker where he'd last seen the woman he loved.

In his head he knew Bill wouldn't answer. The man was dead. He couldn't hear Jared from his resting place beneath a slab of marble. Bill had moved beyond human concerns, presumably to a place without earthly problems.

No one in his right mind would be jealous of a corpse, and Jared reminded himself he had less reason than most to envy Althea's dead fiancé. He, not Bill, was the only man who'd ever shared Althea's bed. He'd been the first to give her a woman's pleasure.

Jared didn't believe in ghosts.

So, why was he standing here, looking for answers from a dead man? Why wasn't he tiptoeing into his house at this moment, sweeping his woman off her feet?

Truth was, Jared was terrified. Scared stiff that she'd

throw him out, all because he tended to take things over, to do them his way. He was fearful enough of what he'd find with her that he was standing here in a cemetery, at midnight, tempting whatever disembodied spirits might be lurking on the gentle mountain breeze.

"Cain?"

Jared thought his imagination was working overtime until he saw Jim stride toward him. "You damn near scared me to death," he said when Althea's brother faced him from the other side of Bill's grave.

"What the hell are you doing in the graveyard this time of night?"

Jared shrugged. "Thinking. How about you?"

"I was working late on a set of custom cabinets. I saw your car, thought I'd make sure you're okay."

"I'm fine." Jared hesitated, then continued. "Have you heard from Althea this week?"

Jim shook his head. "Not since Monday. I've been spending all my time on this job. What's up?"

Suddenly the surroundings seemed to close in on Jared. "Why don't we go over to the cars?" He turned, had to fight to walk, not run.

Jim followed. When they got to the parking lot, he leaned against his van and gestured toward the grave they'd just left. "Is my sister worried about being untrue to him? She shouldn't be. Last thing Bill would want would be for Althea to spend the rest of her life mourning for him."

"I think it's more that she's worried about being true to herself."

"Huh?"

Jared realized what he'd just told Jim didn't make

good sense. "Althea believes I want to take away her independence," he said to clarify his previous statement.

"She shouldn't ever have gone away to college, got those fancy women's lib ideas." Jim shook his head, as if the idea of a woman being her own boss was too much for him to digest. "What does she want, to keep her little quilt shop after you two get hitched?"

"I don't mind if she wants to keep the shop. It's that she wanted to get that craft co-op off the ground by herself. I made a big mistake when I thought she'd be happy that I bought some land and arranged to have a building put up for her."

Jim snorted. "How did she think she'd get it for herself? Local businessmen weren't all that interested in coughing up the money to get it started, even when Bill was pushing the idea. When he died, so did the co-op. Until you stepped in, that is, and got the ball rolling again."

All of a sudden Jared could see why doing for herself had gotten so important to Althea. Her own brother seemed not to realize what she had to offer or how much she'd accomplished by making a success of her shop in a few short years. "Yeah, I got it rolling all right." He had a sinking feeling Althea might be comparing him to a steamroller.

"I need to get some sleep if I'm gonna get up early in the morning and finish those cabinets. You gotta lay the law down, Jared. Let my sister know you're the boss." With that final word, Jim climbed into his van and drove away.

Jared sat in his car for a long time, mulling over what Jim had said. Finally he backed out onto the highway, headed home.

Althea had to be at his place, he figured, since he hadn't seen her Pathfinder in front of her cabin or the quilt shop. He feared the worst, yet hoped for the best as he downshifted and followed the winding gravel road up the side of Big Bear Mountain.

Althea stared at the digital clock on the nightstand, groaned. It was after one o'clock in the morning. If she didn't get to sleep, she'd be a zombie. She set down the box with the heart-shaped jewel. She'd been holding it for heaven knew how long. Disgusted with herself for letting this impossible situation get her down, she stretched out on the bed.

A crunching noise made her sit up and listen. When the sound got louder, she could also hear the distinctive roar of a powerful engine. Someone was driving up the mountain. Jared? It had to be. No one else drove a car that sounded like his Mercedes.

She hadn't expected him until tomorrow—later today, she amended when she thought about what time it was. She'd expected to have waking time away from here to shore up her resolve to let him go. Suddenly cold in spite of the long T-shirt she had on, she grabbed the blanket and wrapped herself in it.

A door closed softly downstairs. A light switch clicked in the silence while his footsteps fell—at first sharply on the oak plank floor, then muted. He must have been crossing the living room with its braided rug.

"No!"

Hearing his anguished cry made her drop the blanket and leap out of bed. She moved to the landing at the top of the stairs. There he was, hugging the finished quilt against his wide, muscled chest. Tears dampened his cheeks.

This wasn't the way she'd imagined seeing him with his quilt. Not at all. "Jared?"

His gaze intense, he raked her from head to toe. His eyes reflected the color of the forest greens in his quilt, along with fear, hope, love—all the emotions that were flooding her own heart.

And she sensed his desire, banked but burning bright. It touched her, heated her blood, and made her tingle. Suddenly she wished she were wearing armor, or at least something more substantial than one of his old T-shirts.

Jared was all wrong for her. As wrong as if he'd landed on the mountainside from some distant planet. She wasn't the woman he needed, and he wasn't the man to fulfill her dreams. His idea of caring was taking over, while hers was nurturing.

She could repeat her warnings to herself. She could embellish on them until they became a litany. Still she couldn't stop herself from holding out her arms and welcoming him home. She couldn't squelch the love that welled up in her heart, any more than she could douse the passion he set off in her belly.

In slow motion, he climbed the spiral stairs. He came close. Closer. Then he was beside her, wrapping her in his quilt and crushing her against his rock-hard body. He tasted her, first gently and then fiercely, until she couldn't tell where his breath ended and hers began.

How could she give him up? She couldn't, not now, in the dark of night when he silently promised love, passion, and a beating heart to share the uncertainties they'd face tomorrow. When Jared scooped her into his arms and carried her to his bed, Althea uttered not a word of protest. Hands tangled in clothes, desperate to reach bare skin. Murmurs and moans mingled, accompaniment for her desperate wish for things to be other than as they were, for Jared to be the simple man she'd wanted, not the millionaire tycoon who thought his wealth could make his every dream come true. Althea reached out, touched him as she feared she'd never do again.

With each caress, she gave him her love. With every kiss, she made him a promise. She might not have him, but she'd have no other man. She'd spend her life alone in the mountains, go old and gray, pining for Jared Cain.

Gently, so gently, he nudged her legs apart. With tender care, he entered her, made them as one. A sob came up in Althea's throat, but she swallowed it. They were making memories, memories that would have to sustain her over the long, lonely years to come.

He brushed a lone tear from her cheek, gathered her more closely to his heart. He would win Althea, make up to her for Jim and her father—and Bill. Damn Bill anyhow. Softly, he whispered her name, and it sounded like a prayer.

Maybe it was. *Please, God*, he thought. *Let me open up and tell Althea what's in my heart. Don't let it be too late.*

Her arms tightened around his waist, pulled him close. Their hearts beat in unison, slow and steady as the rhythm he set within her soft, giving body. He felt the pressure build and crest inside her once, then again. The third time, he joined her.

But he wouldn't let her go. All through the night he held her.

And he prayed.

Murmured words of love, of promises they'd made in the throes of passion and confirmed in its hazy contented afterglow, rang in Jared's head the next morning as he watched Althea sleep. Surely she'd stay with him and become the missing half of him he'd searched for, unknowing, for longer than he could remember.

He stared at the quilt, her reason for agreeing to come back here after she said he'd violated her trust. Now that he was getting up, he draped it over her to keep her warm. With any kind of luck, they'd spend years together, cuddling under the Flying Geese that had brought Althea to him in the first place.

He'd said the words he'd never voiced before. He'd opened his heart to her, and left himself vulnerable on the outside where he'd been unprotected inside all along. He could lose his company, all the material things he'd managed to amass, and still survive. If he lost Althea, it would be losing the best part of himself.

She'd looked so tired last night when he came home, he'd decided to let her sleep away Sunday morning. Mentally, he scrapped his half-formed plan to take her to services at the church next to the cemetery, to let her neighbors see them together and begin to think of them as a couple. She needed rest. Besides, they needed time to talk, somewhere other than in bed.

His gaze settled on a neat row of open jeweler's boxes on the nightstand. His gifts, the ones he'd ordered as the result of a drunken inspiration.

Curious, he picked up the boxes one by one. What had Althea's reaction been? he wondered as he looked at each glittering jewel. He imagined he'd find out soon enough.

He pulled on clean underwear, then grabbed a shirt and jeans. Quietly, he left the bedroom and went downstairs to shave and dress.

Coffee in hand a few minutes later, he went out on the porch. Sunlight filtered through the tall trees, casting dappled shadows across the rough-hewn cedar floor. Tired yet too wired to sleep, he leaned back in a chair and listened to water tumble over the boulders in the stream beneath his feet.

"Jared?" Althea's soft call jarred him from his idle thoughts.

"I'm out here, sweetheart."

"Good morning." She set her coffee on the table next to him, then sat down on the bench next to the porch rail. "I guess you saw I finished your quilt."

"It looks good, especially with you underneath it." A chill slithered into his gut. It sounded as though she were getting ready to say goodbye.

"I love you. But I don't think we're going to make it together," she told him.

He tried to smile, as though he couldn't take her seriously. "Why?"

"We're too different. Different worlds, different ideas about what's important. I feel out of place in your world, Jared."

"My world's yours, sweetheart. It's you." He stood and held his arms out to her.

She got up, then took a sidestep away from him. "Listen to me. Please. You make me uncomfortable.

Your wealth, the way you buy whatever it is you get a notion to, intimidates me."

"You're talking about the jewelry. Althea, the aquamarines reminded me of your eyes—"

"Not just the jewelry, although that's part of it. The land for the co-op. The brand new building that's going up on that land as we speak. Even small things like the quilting frame you bought. And the quilt itself. You want something, so you buy it. No thought, no deliberation. I can't live with that."

"You want me to become a miser?" Damn it, he'd worked hard to get to where he could spend money as he saw fit without worrying about it.

"Oh, Jared. You don't understand."

"No. I don't. I've known women who'd pretend love they didn't feel to get themselves a rich man, but you're the first one I've come across who'd throw away love because the guy you fell for happens to have a lot of money."

"It's not the money, Jared; it's the way you think. The way I think. How we live, what's important to us. We're just too different." Althea took his hand, brought it to her lips.

Her breath tickled his knuckles, and he hardened his resolve to overcome her arguments about their future. "What's important to me, sweetheart, is you. Us. The kind of life we can have together. Damn it, I'm not going to say I'm sorry for helping you realize your vision for the co-op. Or for giving you whatever gifts I can afford that I want you to have. I'm not about to apologize for having worked hard and made my dream for Cain Software a reality."

"I don't want you to apologize. Jared, you've made

yourself a world out there, but it's a world where I don't feel comfortable. A world where you can open your wallet and make things happen that most men can't. I'm a simple country girl. I don't belong in the world you've made for yourself."

"My roots are here, same as yours."

"I've tried to believe that. I've tried to tell myself you've come home to these mountains. To me. But Jared, you've moved a million miles from Big Bear Mountain in every way that counts." She sounded sad, as if she'd made up her mind to walk away.

He had to say something, persuade her to stay. "But—"

"You know it's true."

"Come with me." He took her hand, pulled her down the steps behind him.

"Where are we going?"

"Just come. There's something I want you to see."

Holding her hand, Jared headed up the steep pathway that led to the summit of the mountain. As they went higher, the path narrowed. A blood vessel throbbed in his temple. He had to make her understand. If he couldn't, he'd lose the first real love he'd ever had. He'd lose Althea.

When they finally stopped at the end of the path, Althea tried to catch her breath. Jared still held her hand as if he thought she'd bolt given half a chance.

"Look. These are my roots. This is where I spent the first twelve years of my life." He inclined his head toward what appeared to be an odd-shaped, overgrown clearing.

She caught her breath, then looked around. The stone and cement foundation of a tiny cabin stood, its rotting walls caved in on themselves and what remained of a thick tree trunk. A few yards away lay the carcass of a rotted truck tire. Remnants of a rope still hung from it.

"I used to play for hours under that old tree. Thought I'd died and gone to heaven when Dad hung that tire up so I could swing out over the gully."

Once he must have dreamed simple dreams, found pleasure in nature and amusements less complex than the elaborate games that had made him his fortune. Althea watched a wealth of emotions flash across his handsome face. Nostalgia. Pain. Love. It was as though he'd raised a curtain on his soul, set his feelings free.

Althea glanced at the cabin ruins that seemed almost obscene against the background of a brilliant sky and majestic evergreens. "You found that quilt square inside those ruins."

"Yes." He touched her cheek, so softly she might have mistaken his fingers for the breeze if she hadn't been looking his way. "There was nothing else. Just that square and one old rotten tire to show for all the years Cains lived on Big Bear Mountain."

Althea took his hand and brushed it across her lips. "There's you, Jared."

"Yeah. I may have been crazy, but I thought of this miserable place as home. I kept picturing Mom working on her quilts inside and Dad taking me to pan for gold—" He paused, and gestured toward the jumble of rocks and rotting timbers. "Smiling. They both seemed happy all the time. Mom never smiled after we went away."

"I'm sorry. I understand how you must have felt."

His expression turned fierce. "You don't have the faintest idea how I felt. I was twelve years old, damn it. Twelve years old. No time to cry because I'd lost my dad. No chance to remember the fun we'd had, because I was too busy trying to step into the shoes he hadn't filled even when he was alive, but that I'd been too dumb to realize needed filling. Shoes I couldn't fill because I was nothing but a worthless little kid. Somebody my mom had to take care of."

"Jared—"

"No. Don't say it. If you had any idea how useless I felt when I helped Mom haul the pitifully few things we had down this mountain, you'd understand why I made a vow I'd never end up dirt poor. I'd never be a worthless dreamer like my old man."

Althea wished she'd known Jared then, before he'd lost his childhood and learned some folks measured pleasure in terms of its price.

"You must have missed this place something fierce." She looked away from him, at the cabin's ruins, because it hurt too much to watch him suffer.

He knelt on the ground, rubbed a hand across the carcass of the tire. "I missed what I'd made of it in my mind."

Even before time and the elements had reduced it to a pile of rubble, the home Jared had kept in his heart for all these years couldn't have been much more than a couple of tiny rooms. But apparently he'd made it a symbol of all he'd had and lost. His childhood and his sense of belonging.

"I bought this mountain and came here searching for something. I thought this would be it. The home I remembered from when I was a boy. But it wasn't. Wouldn't have been, even if nature had preserved the place the way I remembered it."

He stood, then moved toward the ruined cabin. When he stopped outside what Althea imagined must have been the front door, he turned and looked at her.

"Know what I finally figured out? Home wasn't a place; it was family. Love. Mom, Dad, me. We'd have been home in an Atlanta mansion or a condo on the beach as much as we were here. Money doesn't matter when you've got love, sweetheart."

Tears threatened to spill down Althea's cheeks, but she blinked them back. She wanted to believe him, take a chance that love could bridge the gap between her world and his. But despite his protests, the truth was that their worlds were light years apart.

He walked over to the edge of the clearing, then bent and plucked a delicate wildflower. Never looking anywhere but straight at her, he came back and smiled as he handed her the pale yellow blossom.

"Here. This is my heart. It belongs to you. It breaks easily, so please take care of it."

The velvety petals fluttered in the breeze, as if to remind her how fragile they were—how easily they could be destroyed.

How easily she could lose the love he brought her—the heady emotions she hadn't thought she wanted ever to risk feeling again.

"I don't want to hurt you," she said softly, holding his sober gaze as she hugged the flower to her breast.

He smiled. "Then believe in us. Give us a chance. Take the same kind of pleasure when I give you diamonds as you're taking in that little flower I just picked and handed to you. They're both beautiful. And the message I'm sending you with them is the same."

The kernel of insecurity inside Althea burst into bloom, made it hard for her to breathe. If only she could conquer it.

But she couldn't. "I want to believe we can make it work, Jared. So much. But I'm afraid. Afraid you'll get tired of me, want someone—"

"Hush." He put a hand gently over her mouth.

She loved the way his eyes reflected the colors around him. Now they seemed more amber than green against the backdrop of blue sky and russet earth. Warm. Full of love and hope.

"Listen to me, Althea. I've never wanted anybody the way I want you, and that's the truth. You satisfy me in every way. You make me whole. Losing you would be like losing the better half of me."

Althea sighed. She couldn't keep fighting him when that meant fighting herself as well. "I can't help loving you."

"Enough to risk marrying me?"

She nodded. Risk was the operative word, but she couldn't deny her heart. "I even love you enough to put up with your taking over and deciding what I need before I even know myself. I'd appreciate, though, if you'd ask before you do something else on the grand scale of the co-op."

He laid his hand over his heart. With the other hand, he retrieved something from a pocket in his jeans.

His expression serious, he took her hand. "Let me put this back where it belongs," he said, as he slid her engagement ring back on her finger.

"About those other . . ."

"Those trinkets I've been sending for the past few days? Pretend they came out of boxes of Cracker Jack, and just say thanks."

Althea started to make a sarcastic reply, but she held it back. She could live with Jared's buying her extravagant gifts if that gave him pleasure, but she wouldn't stand for him to barge in and take over projects she needed to do for herself.

"All right. Thank you." She returned his smile with one of her own. "They're beautiful."

"There, that wasn't too difficult, was it?"

"No. But, Jared, I won't thank you for going behind my back and arranging to build the co-op facility."

"I'm sorry, sweetheart. Not for anything I did, but for not talking over my plans with you before going ahead with them. I'll try to remember you don't like surprises like that." His smile seemed almost angelic, but she noticed a wicked twinkle in his eyes.

And if she believed he wouldn't barge right in the next time he wanted to do something he thought he'd do better or faster than she could do for herself, she'd be a good prospect for a con artist who was selling oceanfront property in Iowa.

But Althea grinned back at him. She'd watch Jared, enjoy every inch of the view. She'd given him her love, but she'd be careful to hold onto a piece of herself.

She put her hand in his, her heart in his care. "Let's go home."

TWENTY-FIVE

Three weeks later, they got married quietly, the way Althea wanted. Jared watched his bride of less than two hours as she disappeared into the bathroom.

He stripped off the gray suit he'd worn to the wedding and hung it in the closet, then crawled into the big oak bed under the quilt Althea had finished while their future had been uncertain. Idly, as he listened to water pound against the shower walls, he traced around a square of the quilt with one finger. He recalled his mom's words from long ago.

The geese fly away from the mountains every fall, the way we're going to do. Someday, though, they'll come back.

Each small stitch abraded his fingertips. They reminded him of the long hours and the love Althea had invested to fulfill the dream his mother had put into his head so long ago.

God, how he loved Althea—and how he wished she'd hurry. How long could it take for her to do whatever it was she was doing in the bathroom and come to him?

His wife. Saying the vows that joined them hadn't brought terror to his throat the way he'd always thought it would. A kind of peace had come over him this afternoon when she walked down the aisle to him. Now gentle anticipation was giving way to impatience. Impatience for her to join him under the Flying Geese so they could seal the promises they'd made.

They'd made love a hundred times, knew each other's bodies better than their own, yet tonight was special. Jared rubbed his palm along his jaw. He'd shaved before the wedding. No matter. Folding the quilt back, he got up and hurried downstairs. Tonight of all nights, he couldn't chafe Althea's tender skin. He showered again, then hurried back to their room and crawled in bed.

What was taking Althea so long?

In the bathroom, Althea breathed in the scent of woods violets she'd used in the shower as she slid an old-fashioned embroidered muslin nightgown over her head. She smiled when she looked at the platinum band Jared had slid on her finger next to the big diamond solitaire she still hadn't gotten used to wearing.

He was trying. He'd even let her go with him to select their wedding bands, and he'd kept his complaints to himself when she'd insisted on the simple matching bands.

Until she looked at Jared as Jim led her down the aisle today and saw the unconditional love etched on his handsome features, she had been afraid. Now she was ready for whatever the future might bring. Smiling at her blurred image in the steamed-up mirror, Althea fastened the chain that held a ruby heart around her neck.

Recalling nights she'd come to Jared as naked as a newborn, Althea slipped into her nightgown, then opened the door. She shivered, and not just from the cool air in the room. The sight of her husband, propped up on a pile of pillows in their big oak bed under the quilt that had brought them together, took her breath away.

His eyes reflected the greens in the quilt. The intensity of his gaze as he looked her over head to toe made her feel as though he were seeing every inch of her through the modest gown Trina had made from a century-old pattern and given her for her wedding night.

"Come here."

She took a step closer. The muscles in his arms and chest rippled as he sat up all the way and let the quilt settle in his lap. Tanned and fit, Jared Cain in bed was a sight designed to turn a woman to jelly. It was obvious he was naked beneath the Flying Geese.

Althea felt his heated gaze clear down to her toes. At the same time he swept aside the quilt and made a spot for her beside him, she lifted the hem of the concealing gown and brought the garment over her head. It slid onto the floor, and she slid into her husband's arms.

The sheets felt soft against her skin, warm from her husband's body heat. He touched her as gently as though she were made of porcelain, as reverently as if this would be their first time making love.

Slowly, like virgin lovers, they explored each other's heat. She etched the masculine angle of his jaw and tested the texture of silky hair on the taut, satiny skin of his chest before she moved her hand lower to explore the steely, pulsing proof of his desire.

"Stop. I can't wait if you . . ."

"Don't wait," she whispered. His need stoked hers,

fueled the flame inside her. She lay back to make room for him, then welcomed him home.

Slowly, then faster when she urged him on, he stroked her. The tension built, then burst in an explosion of sensation that was familiar, yet new. For a long time they lay together, savoring the afterglow.

Althea felt Jared pull the quilt over her shoulders when she started to shiver.

"Thank you, sweetheart," he said, as he brushed a strand of her hair back from her cheek.

She cupped his cheeks between her hands. "My pleasure." And it had been, was, and would be for the rest of their lives.

His arms went around her, held her close. "God, how I love you."

He could say the words now, without hesitating. And she had no problem returning them in kind. "No more than I love you."

"My wife. I'm the luckiest man alive." He paused, blew gently on her ear.

She gave him a playful squeeze. "No luckier than I am to have you. I'm glad you talked me into spending the first night of our honeymoon at home."

"Me, too," he told her. "For the first time, I feel as if the wanderer in me has finally settled in. I've come home. And I couldn't be happier."

BOOK YOUR PLACE ON OUR WEBSITE AND MAKE THE READING CONNECTION!

We've created a customized website just for our very special readers, where you can get the inside scoop on everything that's going on with Zebra, Pinnacle and Kensington books.

When you come online, you'll have the exciting opportunity to:

- View covers of upcoming books
- Read sample chapters
- Learn about our future publishing schedule (listed by publication month *and author*)
- Find out when your favorite authors will be visiting a city near you
- Search for and order backlist books from our online catalog
- Check out author bios and background information
- Send e-mail to your favorite authors
- Meet the Kensington staff online
- Join us in weekly chats with authors, readers and other guests
- Get writing guidelines
- AND MUCH MORE!

**Visit our website at
http://www.zebrabooks.com**

COMING IN MARCH FROM ZEBRA BOUQUET ROMANCES

#37 LOVE ON THE RUN by Leigh Greenwood
__(0-8217-6531-0, **$3.99**) Accused of selling company secrets to the competition, investment banker Claire Dalton is desperate to stay out of jail. Eric Sterling doubts her innocence—until a savage attack convinces him that someone wants her dead. Now, his need to protect her stirs up passionate desires he finds hard to control.

#38 LITTLE WHITE LIES by Judy Gill
__(0-8217-6532-9, **$3.99**) Doug Fountain needs a fiancée—for a month only. That will be enough time for his grandfather to hand over the family business to a "suitable heir." Doug hopes to find a woman who will go along with his scheme . . . if he promises her the right deal. And that deal definitely doesn't include love—or does it?

#39 LOOKING FOR PERFECTION by Valerie Kirkwood
__(0-8217-6533-7, **$3.99**) From the moment Mitch Ballard meets high spirited Zoe, there are downright fireworks. But his life is complicated enough right now, and the last thing he needs is to tumble head over heels in love. If only his heart didn't find her so absolutely irresistable.

#40 THE LAST TRUE COWBOY by Mary Schramski
__(0-8217-6534-5, **$3.99**) A heartbreaking marriage to a bull rider taught Beth Morris the hard way that family comes last for thrill-seeking men. So when handsome rider Trace Barlow shows up at her ranch, she has no intention of giving this reckless cowboy the time of day. Can Trace convince Beth that the only prize he's interested in winning is her heart

---

Call toll free **1-888-345-BOOK** to order by phone, use this coupon to order by mail, or order online at **www.kensingtonbooks.com**.

Name _____
Address _____
City _____ State _____ Zip_____
Please send me the books I have checked above.
I am enclosing $_____
Plus postage and handling* $_____
Sales tax (in New York and Tennessee only) $_____
Total amount enclosed $_____
*Add $2.50 for the first book and $.50 for each additional book.
Send check or money order (no cash or CODs) to:
Kensington Publishing Corp., Dept. CO, 850 Third Avenue, New York, NY 10022
Prices and numbers subject to change without notice.
All orders subject to availability. All books available 3/1/00.
Visit our web site at **www.kensingtonbooks.com**.

Put a Little Romance in Your Life With
Fern Michaels

_Dear Emily	0-8217-5676-1	$6.99US/$8.50CAN
_Sara's Song	0-8217-5856-X	$6.99US/$8.50CAN
_Wish List	0-8217-5228-6	$6.99US/$7.99CAN
_Vegas Rich	0-8217-5594-3	$6.99US/$8.50CAN
_Vegas Heat	0-8217-5758-X	$6.99US/$8.50CAN
_Vegas Sunrise	1-55817-5983-3	$6.99US/$8.50CAN
_Whitefire	0-8217-5638-9	$6.99US/$8.50CAN

Call toll free **1-888-345-BOOK** to order by phone or use this coupon to order by mail.
Name_____
Address_____
City _____ State _____ Zip_____
Please send me the books I have checked above.
I am enclosing $_____
Plus postage and handling* $_____
Sales tax (in New York and Tennessee) $_____
Total amount enclosed $_____
*Add $2.50 for the first book and $.50 for each additional book.
Send check or money order (no cash or CODs) to:
Kensington Publishing Corp., 850 Third Avenue, New York, NY 10022
Prices and Numbers subject to change without notice.
All orders subject to availability.
Check out our website at **www.kensingtonbooks.com**

Simply the Best...
Katherine Stone

__**Bel Air**	**$6.99**US/**$7.99**CAN
0-8217-5201-4	
__**The Carlton Club**	**$6.99**US/**$7.99**CAN
0-8217-5204-9	
__**Happy Endings**	**$6.99**US/**$7.99**CAN
0-8217-5250-2	
__**Illusions**	**$6.99**US/**$7.99**CAN
0-8217-5247-2	
__**Love Songs**	**$6.99**US/**$7.99**CAN
0-8217-5205-7	
__**Promises**	**$6.99**US/**$7.99**CAN
0-8217-5248-0	
__**Rainbows**	**$6.99**US/**$7.99**CAN
0-8217-5249-9	

Call toll free **1-888-345-BOOK** to order by phone, use this coupon to order by mail, or order online at **www.kensingtonbooks.com**.
Name_____
Address _____
City_____ State _____ Zip _____
Please send me the books I have checked above.
I am enclosing $_____
Plus postage and handling* $_____
Sales tax (in New York and Tennessee only) $_____
Total amount enclosed $_____
*Add $2.50 for the first book and $.50 for each additional book.
Send check or money order (no cash or CODs) to:
Kensington Publishing Corp., Dept C.O., 850 Third Avenue, 16th Floor, New York, NY 10022
Prices and numbers subject to change without notice.
All orders subject to availability.
Visit our website at **www.kensingtonbooks.com**.